Woman Alive

INTRODUCED BY

Graham Norton

Woman Alive

Susan Ertz

MANDERLEY PRESS

Named for the house in Daphne du Maurier's novel *Rebecca*, Manderley Press finds forgotten or out-of-print books that were deeply inspired by a building, city or landmark, and brings those lost publications back to life for a contemporary audience.

We love selling our titles through bookshops around the world, and we especially delight in posting them to customers from our offices here in London. Ordering from us directly makes a huge difference to our independent press, allowing us to re-invest in future titles and exciting literary projects. As a thank you, we include matching bookmarks with each title, created exclusively for manderleypress.com readers.

The books all feature a specially commissioned introduction and cover, with both the author and the artist chosen for their connections to the places at the heart of each title. Cover artwork is also available to purchase, as signed giclée art prints.

Every Manderley Press title is exquisitely produced as a small hardback edition, printed on luxurious paper, and bound in real cloth, with head and tail bands too.

For more information and a full list of published titles, please visit us at www.manderleypress.com

Manderley Press

This hardback edition published in 2026 by Manderley Press
www.manderleypress.com

This book was first published by Appleton-Century Company Incorporated, New York, 1936

ISBN: 978-1-0686613-6-5

Typeset in Chiswick and Chiswick Sans by Commercial Type
Designed by Myfanwy Vernon-Hunt, This-Side
Printed and bound by Finidr, s.r.o.

EU Authorised Representative:
EAS Europe - Mustamäe tee 50, 10621 Tallinn, Estonia
gpsr.requests@easproject.com

MIX
Paper | Supporting responsible forestry
FSC® C014138

Manderley Press

CONTENTS

INTRODUCTION

Graham Norton

Success seems so real when it is happening. The Booker Prize, the Oscar for Best Picture, when such gongs are handed out, the legacy of the winners seems assured, and yet a glance back over the recipients of rave reviews and bestseller lists, reveals names we have long forgotten, books and films we struggle to remember. It seems the passage of time has a different measure for success than we do in the here and now.

Those were my thoughts as I picked up a faded box-set containing the original ten Penguin Classics that had been issued in 1935. I was browsing the book tent at the annual church fete in Durrus, a small village near my home in West Cork. The dusty Penguin orange seemed incongruous amongst the gleaming piles, of Maeve Binchys, Jeffrey Archers and a surprising number by Leon Uris.

Glancing at the ten slim volumes, some names immediately jumped out – Agatha Christie, Ernest Hemingway, Dorothy L. Sayers – but others had clearly not proved to be such classics.

Who was Mary Webb? E.H. Young anyone? Compton Mackenzie might be a familiar name, but have any of us read *Carnival?* I decided that the little box-set would be a welcome addition to a house where visitors had plenty of rainy days to read, so popped it in my basket.

When I got home, I opted not to reach for one of the familiar names, but instead chose *Madame Claire* by Susan Ertz, which had been originally published in 1923. I was naturally dubious – after all, history had chosen to allow this title to fall behind the back of the bookcase while keeping Agatha and Ernest front and centre.

It turned out that history was an old fool. The book was an utter delight. A wealthy old woman living in a Kensington hotel, trying to solve all the problems of her family and beyond. The tone is all charming froth, but Ertz still manages to tackle the sorrow of aging and the heartbreak of lost love with enormous empathy and gravitas. It is as if she is using the genre of drawing room comedy as a Trojan Horse.

Wanting to know more about Susan Ertz, I turned to the internet, which also seemed to have decided she was not worthy of our attention. Amongst the few available facts I *was* able to find, I was surprised to learn the author of the very British novel I'd just read was born to American parents, albeit in Surrey, England, in 1887. Her youth was divided between Britain and the States. I saw one claim that while in America, she and her siblings managed to survive the great San Francisco earthquake of 1906. Ertz returned to Britain permanently during the First World War, marrying Major John Ronald McCrindle in 1932.

Madame Claire was her first published work, but she went on to be quite prolific, producing twenty-one novels and a collection of short stories. Her last completed novel was released in 1976. Why has she been so completely forgotten? Not the right people to champion her work, dwindling sales, or simply the wrong publisher? It is doubtful we will ever know the truth since, as far as I know, no biography of Susan Ertz has been written. It appears that some of her works were more successful than others. *Madame Claire* had been a slow burn initially but by 1935 had become successful enough to attract the attention of Penguin. *The Proselyte*, 1933, told the story of an English woman moving to Utah to live with the Mormons, and her 1960 novel *In the Cool of the Day,* was turned into a film of the same name staring Jane Fonda and Angela Lansbury. A few years ago, Fonda declared it the worst movie she had ever made.

Then we come to this book, *Woman Alive*. Originally published in serial form as *One Woman Alive,* it is a surprising departure for Ertz. Reading *Madame Claire* I would never have guessed that the same author had also tackled science fiction. The book is essentially a time travel story. A Dr. Selwyn is transported to 1985 where he finds a world where all women are dying due to a gas released during an act of war. He then discovers Stella Morrow, a young woman unaffected by the gas-related malady, and the novel describes what happens to her and the world in the months that follow.

I must admit, I normally struggle with time-travel stories, mostly because of the many inconsistencies and convoluted means of travel. Ertz avoids these problems by neatly dispensing with the science element of her science-fiction story. Selwyn is transported to the future by a sort of Italian mystic or clairvoyant and the doctor doesn't experience the future as himself but rather as the old man he would be in 1985. The younger Selwyn, returned from the future, deals with all the possible contradictions before beginning his account of the adventure.

The heart of this novel, Dr. Selwyn's experiences in the eighties, has the feel of a fable, or morality tale, but Ertz sprinkles in enough eccentricities and foibles to ground the story in an almost plausible reality. The world we encounter where all women are dying is shockingly dark and yet there is a parallel optimism in the author's view of the future. Architecture, education, transport and health are all described as almost utopian. Once Stella Morrow, the only woman alive, finds her voice we discover the real blight on the world: men. Despite all the advances made, there appears to have been no progress in the equality of the sexes. Men remain in charge, and it is under their stewardship that humankind has been brought to the brink of extinction.

This book was clearly inspired, or, at the very least, influenced by the political clouds gathering across Europe in the thirties, but sadly that is also what makes it such a timely read today. Stella Morrow's view of the world is simple and uncompromising but most of all it is sincere. At one point she says of men, *Oh, you strange creatures! So careless of life and of the world, so eager for it to continue! Who can understand you?* This basic question is as pertinent now as it ever was.

Susan Ertz is writing as someone who had lived and volunteered during the First World War. Her message of pacifism is clearly a plea from the heart, but she evidently still has hope for the future. It is interesting to contrast her vision of 1985 with Orwell's *1984*, written in the years following the Second World War. Is it just the difference between a male and female perspective or did that conflict make any sort of optimism much harder?

Having finished this dreamlike book, where women are no longer to be ignored, one final detail astonished me. Dr. Selwyn travels to a very specific time, 15 April 1985. Susan Ertz died on 11 April 1985, just four days short of the future she had dreamt of half a century before. I am so pleased that the clever people at Manderley Press have chosen to reissue this little gem, so that once more Susan Ertz is a woman alive!

Graham Norton, 2026

When I met Ugolino Spero this afternoon in that top-floor room at Number 149B Campden Hill Gardens, I was seeing him for the fourth time.

About three months ago Professor Ladoux asked me to take part in a group sitting. That was just before Spero's illness, and it wasn't altogether a success. I admit that all of us who were there that day – with the exception of Hoffman – received certain impressions and passed through certain brief experiences that had nothing to do with the past or present as we knew it, but when it was all over we weren't able to convince ourselves that Spero had not broken down some of the isolation that normally exists between mind and mind, so that our thoughts and memories flowed from one to another and mingled. In other words, we were inclined to think he had merely produced a set of conditions in which thought-transference was easy and unconscious. And I apologize for saying "merely." If he had, in fact, done this, it was remarkable enough, but it was not what we were after.

In Florence, where he was born, there were scientists, doctors, writers, and even priests who were willing to testify to his extraordinary powers. They claimed that by the exercise of some unknown faculty he could fix his mind upon a place and a period in the future and present to the minds of his sitters a picture of what was going on there – a claim so extravagant that few of our own investigators were willing to give it their serious attention. He himself, it was said, would pass into a state of complete unconsciousness, while his sitters, provided they were able to free their minds of everything but an attitude of quiet expectancy, would receive vivid pictures of happenings which formed no part of their own past lives.

We had agreed to ask Spero, that first day, to let us see something of our own lives fifteen years hence.

The pictures I myself received were all of far-off Eastern places. Now the East, as we all know, is unchanging, or is changing very slowly, and though the scenes I saw – I had never been beyond Marseilles – were new and strange to me, they might, for all I know, be taking place today. Or – and this was the explanation we all preferred – I might have been seeing something already seen by Boyle Hoffman, who has spent eight years in China and five in Japan. Professor Ladoux told us he seemed to be in New York. At any rate, he said he was surrounded by new buildings of considerable height and magnificence such as he had seen in photographs. He couldn't make up his mind, though, whether he had been seeing the New York of the present or the London of the future, as he thought the two might conceivably be somewhat alike. I had spent some months in New York a short time before, and for all I know he might have been receiving those impressions from me. The taxi accident he described was very like the one in which I myself was involved while driving to the Pennsylvania Station one day.

Hoffman got nothing at all. He said his mind just went squirrelling round and round over the small events of the day. Sir Horace Grainger, the president of the Society of Inquirers, said he seemed to be flying very low over an interminable sea. A mist rose up from it, and he was conscious of the continual movement, and of feeling cold and afraid. We couldn't account for this on the grounds of thought-transference, none of us having flown further than to Glasgow and back. (Spero might have done so. It didn't occur to us to ask him then and I forgot to ask him on later occasions.)

Anyway, we weren't at all satisfied with the results obtained, and it seemed to me folly to attempt other group sittings. He must take us singly, I said, in order to rule out the possibility that the impressions we received came to us from one another.

Then, soon after that, Spero had a nervous breakdown and spent over a month in a nursing home. I went to see him twice, and the second time he said that as soon as he was better he would like me to come to him for a private sitting. He said he thought we should have very good results. He was very urgent about it, and kept repeating:

"Please, please, Dr. Selwyn, say you will come! Say you will come!"

It was what I wanted above everything. Spero interested me enormously, and there was, I felt, a curious sort of understanding between us. Also I knew he was a sick man and might not live to give many more sittings. He was a delicate instrument, delicate mentally and physically. He was subject to epileptic fits, had an inherited taint in his blood and a defective lung. He oughtn't to have been living in England at all, but he was a passionate lover of liberty and said that he had found it only in England. He was thin, with a sort of brittle thinness, and frequently ran temperatures of a hundred and one or two. Since living in London he had been constantly in the care of the famous Italian specialist, Dr. Luigi Bianchetti.

Spero has always given me the impression of knowing, sadly enough, his own uniqueness; of being as lonely and as isolated from the world of men as one planet is from other planets. He had lived in London for some years and spoke English well. He had lost his father and two elder brothers in the Great War, his father at the capture of Gorizia, his two brothers at Caporetto. He was known to be a burning, ardent lover of peace. It was almost, he told me, the whole of his religion – that men should come to realize their brotherhood; that men should cease to inflict death on men. Dr. Bianchetti had strongly advised him to give up his sittings, but Spero had pleaded with him to be allowed at least one more.

"I tell him," he said to me in the nursing home, "that I have found a spirit so much in sympathy with mine that I cannot die happy till I have seen what we can do together."

I begged him not to take the risk, but his mind was made up. He had that great strength of will often possessed by the moribund. He looked at me with such a powerfully pleading gaze that I gave in, unable to resist the urgency in those remarkable eyes. We arranged for the sitting to take place today, April 15th, at the premises of the Society of Inquirers in Campden Hill Gardens. I thought it wise to tell Bianchetti, and he promised to look in about seven and see how Spero had stood the strain.

I was there, in the top-floor room, a few minutes before the appointed time, and when I heard the sound of the lift I went out into the hall.

When I saw Spero I thought, "There'll be no sitting today," for he looked dangerously weak and ill – all black and white, like a man on a screen. I gave him my arm and he leaned on it, looking gratefully up at me. More than ever I felt the charm of that delicate, sombre, Dantesque face.

He lay down on the sofa, and I spread a rug over him and arranged cushions under his head. It was a most unlovely day, with a low, dingy sky, like a dirty dishcloth, and a cruel, gusty east wind. I turned the gas fire full on, for he was shivering, but he talked quite happily, even gaily, and laughed at my solicitude.

"This is nothing, my friend, nothing. I am much better today than yesterday, and I will be better still tomorrow."

We talked for about half an hour. He explained to me some of his theories about time. He said, among other things, that he had been greatly interested in Mr. Dunne's books, *An Experiment in Time*, and *The Serial Universe*. He told me that the first book had suggested to his mind a certain possibility that he had not before taken into consideration, and which somewhat complicated his work.

This was the presence, in time, of What-Might-Be, coexisting (though never actually encountered by us) with What-Is, or What-Will-Be. It had caused him, he said, some doubt and confusion, but he believed that his own powers would be too weak to enable his mind to travel through the trackless forests of What-Might-Be; that What-Will-Be, lying along the road actually to be traversed by mankind, would be far more readily accessible to him.

He believed that he became, in a state of trance or catalepsy, a part of the mind of Dunne's "Universal" or "Synthetic Observer," and that he could then transmit his power of observation to other minds sensitive enough to receive it.

I also had read these books, and had been as fascinated by them as anyone must be who has given himself the trouble of trying to follow their brilliant theorizing. Spero said that for years he had been more or less aware of the truth of Dunne's discoveries, but, not having had the benefits of scientific or mathematical training, and lacking, he said with a smile, Dunne's genius, he had never been able to give clear and logical expression to his beliefs.

When he said to me, "Where shall we go, my friend?" I felt all the excitement of a man who is about to fly over the South Pole, or to ascend into the stratosphere. But I had my answer ready, for I had thought of little else all day.

"I would like you to show me," I said, "a year in my own life fifty years hence, if I am still alive. If I am not alive, let me be an observer, if you can, of what is happening here in London at that date. Am I asking too much?"

"April 15th, 1985," he murmured. "We will see, we will see."

You may think it presumptuous of me to imagine that I might be alive and aware at eighty-eight, but I have always believed that not only would I live to a good old age, but that science, within the next twenty years, would find means of prolonging all human life far be yond its present limits. I, personally, would consider this – in a world not made horrible by war – an inestimable boon and blessing, but on this point everyone is entitled to his own opinion.

I drew my chair close to the sofa where Spero lay, and took his frail hand.

Ever since I was a boy I have been able to empty my mind at will ... to suspend thought. My aunt, Wanda Vines, was one of the greatest of mediums as well as a close student of Indian mysticism. I have a photograph – I never actually saw this happen, though my parents, I believe, often did – of stout Aunt Wanda levitating herself out of the dining-room window of a house we lived in near Reigate. But I learnt a good deal from her in one way and another about mental control. I imagine it was partly this that made Spero anxious to work with me, for without it, owing to the mind's little preoccupations, much is lost.

Spero closed his eyes and I stared into the gas fire. He presently began to jerk and twitch a good deal, though not violently, and sighed very heavily five or six times. That was all. I found the faint hissing of the fire very soothing, and its brightness fixed and held my attention. Presently a sort of film came over my eyes. It dropped down over them like a slow grey curtain. I ceased to see outwardly and began to see inwardly. Then it ceased to be seeing and became living, experiencing. My recollections of the happenings I am about to describe are as sharp, if not sharper, than any I have known in the flesh. I was, in fact, experiencing them in the flesh as a living, breathing man of eighty-eight. I can recall with extreme vividness the feeling of those pavements under my feet, the touch of hands, the smell of grass and flowers and perfumes and human beings and materials. I can recall with perfect ease the excitement of the time, the pity, wonder, horror, joy – all the countless sensations of living. In fact, my mind seemed far keener, far more aware, than it is now. So it is not at all difficult for me to write a detailed account of all that took place. I believe I could write it just as well next month, or next year, or ten years from now; but we think that of dreams, soon after dreaming them, and yet they fade and die, more often than not, soon after waking. So I am taking no risks and am writing this on the evening of April 15th in my own house in Westminster, and will write all night to make sure that nothing is lost of this extraordinary adventure into – well, let us agree to call it the future.

But, before I begin, there is something I must make quite clear to you, something which I shall try not to refer to again, as it would only make for confusion.

Spero was enabling me to experience, out of its proper order in time, a portion of my own future. "Surely," you may say, "all the while you were experiencing it you must have been experiencing something already familiar to you, for you must have been able, as an old man of eighty-eight, to look back upon your life fifty years earlier and remember this sitting with Spero and all that was revealed to you in it. As a part of your past life it must have been still within your memory. Consequently you must have known exactly what was going to happen from day to day; all the scenes you saw and the people you encountered must have been familiar to you. You must have felt that you were living it all for the second time."

This is, in fact, partly true, but only partly. These recollections, so vivid now, yet were, by the time I was eighty-eight, dim, elusive, fragmentary. The feeling that what I was experiencing I had experienced before was intermittent and at no time really convincing. Beyond a feeling that I had known Stella "in some other life," as people say, and beyond an occasional confused impression that the things that were happening had happened to me somewhere before, I was not much troubled by memories. It had all faded, like a dream.

But this written account, you may say. What had become of it? Surely it must have kept your memory of these things alive? My answer is that I don't know what became of it, unless it was destroyed, as so many other things were destroyed – my house among them – in the war. I can tell you no more than that.

It was a strange moment in the world's history into which Spero had projected me.

I first became aware of sound, light, movement, of a soft breeze, of the sun shining. It was very like coming to after a fainting spell. The first thing I actually saw, as the grey curtain thinned and dispersed, was the face of a child. I was looking into it with pity, for it was a terrible face, very old, yet young, and the child could not have been more than five or six. "You poor, poor little thing!" I found myself saying. I put my hand into my pocket and pulled out a bag of sweets. I put some of them into her dirty, claw-like little hand. She was sitting on the edge of the high kerb, and people were passing close to us. Her hand closed on the sweets, and then, as if afraid that they might be taken from her, she scrambled to her feet on weak, uncertain legs, and ran away down the street. She didn't get very far, nor did I think she would. She stumbled, fell, and lay face downwards, and the sweets scattered in all directions. The passers-by paid no attention. They did not go to her aid or call for help. One man stepped over her body and was about to go on, but thought better of it and, turning back, dragged her to the edge of the kerb, out of the way of passing feet.

I went to her, knowing that she was dead, and, turning her over, laid my hand, more or less mechanically, above her heart. Then I took out my handkerchief and spread it over her face. As I did this, some of the people who were passing smiled a little, as people smile at an absurdly sentimental act. I knew it was sentimental, but I was never afraid of sentiment.

Then I went on, knowing that one of the death cars would soon stop to pick her up.

The street in which I found myself that day as a vigorous old man of eighty-eight, and down which I was walking, was Whitehall. It was as familiar to me as it is now, but it would be strange to you. Only the Horse Guards, preserved as a National Monument, remained, and they were almost shouldered out of sight by new buildings. What you would have noticed first, I think, was the brightness, colour, and gaiety of the scene, and, in complete contrast to it, the looks of utter hopelessness and depression on the faces of the people. The buildings were lovely; even now, in the very midst of disaster and universal misery, my eye delighted in their beauty. The use of a malleable glass, easily tinted and almost indestructible, had transformed most cities since the Twenty Days' War of 1950 and the ruin caused by it. The glass, which was translucent, was softly penetrated by daylight, and no room need ever be dark. A suffused, undersea light came in from out-of-doors, and at night the buildings glowed softly and incandescently from the brightness within. I will speak about all this again later; now I must tell you about my walk from the top of Whitehall to my flat in Westminster, overlooking the river, and explain the scenes I saw on my way, and the meaning of them.

I had barely left the dead child when I saw a woman I knew walking towards me. It was Elizabeth Rowley, the wife of the retired Air Marshal, Piers Rowley, and she was walking slowly between her husband and her son, Clement. The poor woman's face was white and wore the universal look of doom. The sickness was already on her, and she knew it, but she was a brave woman and had asked to be taken out for one last stroll about the city she loved so well rather than wait for the end within four walls. I stopped and spoke to them, showing my pity and sympathy only with my eyes, for words were empty and useless. We talked of the beauty of the day; I pressed Elizabeth's hand and went on, and I feared to look behind me, for I had seen that she was on the verge of collapse.

A little further down the street, one of the white death cars was just moving away from the kerb. It was a type of car with which we were only too familiar, and had been designed for use in possible air-raids. (For though we had had thirty-five years of peace, people still demanded vigilance, and, at home, a certain amount of preparedness.) It was a long-bodied car, shaped like an aerial torpedo; its wheels were hidden, and it moved quite soundlessly by what we called air power. For power of every description, from boiling a kettle to propelling the great Transatlantic air liners, was generated from huge central power stations and transmitted by wireless. This was the great innovation of the 'sixties, and we had not yet ceased to marvel at and delight in it.

As a citizen of 1985 I was, of course, perfectly familiar with all the circumstances of the scene about me. And very sadly familiar. I had grown old in London. I had practised medicine there since the age of twenty-eight, had married there at thirty-three, and had now been a widower for three years.

My only son, Derek, lost his life in the Twenty Days' War. His school was destroyed by bombs, and he and over thirty of his school-fellows lost their lives. He was the only child we ever had. Years later, after the discovery of Evitalin, we decided to adopt two baby girls, for it seemed likely then that we would live long enough to see them grow up and establish themselves in life. Their parents had been killed in a flying accident off the coast of Ireland, and we adopted them at the ages of one and a half, and three. They had grown up to be affectionate, intelligent, and beautiful girls, and we loved them as if they had been our own daughters. I had closed Helen's eyes just a week before, and Laura's early the following morning. Helen's last words were:

"We deserve it. We could have prevented this and we didn't. We deserve to die." She made a gallant effort to live until Alan Holderness, her *fiancé*, could reach her, but he was just too late, as people will always be just too late at times, however well we succeed in conquering space. His power-receiver jammed as he was crossing the Atlantic. Luckily for him, it was a calm day and he made a forced sea-landing and repaired the apparatus. But he lost half an hour, and arrived just as they were taking her away.

I thought of those words of Helen's as I walked down Whitehall. Such women as still survived were now objects of doleful interest and pity. Often their looks were wild, their clothing careless. Most of them were companioned by male friends or relations. Some of them laughed and talked hysterically, and their actions were uncontrolled, but this caused no surprise and drew no special attention. One of them, who was walking alone, came up to me. Her cheeks were lavishly rouged and her poor frightened eyes were blackened and her strained lips scarlet. She wore her draperies – women, during this decade, had been dressing rather like the Spartan women – with an air of coquetry in horrid contrast with her ravaged face. She was a little drunk. Not knowing when their moment might come, a great many women used intoxicants to blunt the edge of fear, and who could blame them?

"That's right, grandpa," she said. "Take a good look at me! Here today and gone tomorrow, you know. I'm the last of my familee, I am. The last of my familee. Bye-bye."

I smiled at her and went on. The death cars were plying the streets, constantly on the watch. I had not gone far when two elderly women collapsed a few feet from me. They were alone, and they had no sooner fallen than one of the long white cars drew up at the kerb and two white-clad attendants sprang out and lifted them inside. The doors closed, and the car moved soundlessly away.

I must make these happenings as understandable to you as they were to me.

The United States of Europe, which it had taken so many years of bloodshed and so many more of patient diplomacy to build up, had recently split into two great factions. With unbelievable suddenness one group of nations – of what use to name names here? – attacked the other with thousands of light, fast planes carrying gas bombs, and scattered death over an immense area. These planes had been designed for civil flying, and it had for some time been the proud boast of Mr. Jorgensen, the President of the U.S.E., that there was not a war plane in the whole of Europe! A new gas had been secretly manufactured by the attackers against which the people attacked had no defence. It was called, from its greenish-grey colour – it was not, like most gases, invisible – celadon gas, and it poisoned as well as burned. The destruction of property had ceased to be one of the objects of war; only the destruction of life was aimed at.

England was outside the United States of Europe, having, with the whole of her Empire, joined with America in a League of English-Speaking Peoples. The League, horrified by this act of savagery, prepared to punish the makers of war, but before the counter-attack could even be organized the appalling consequences of those thousands and thousands of deaths from celadon gas began to be felt.

The bodies of those it killed generated a disease – a sort of by-product of the gas itself which proved to be highly contagious and invariably fatal, but – and this was the fact with which the entire world was now faced – fatal only to women. Within twelve hours of the launching of that brief war, which lasted only eight, women began to drop dead in the streets, in their houses, in the fields, in aeroplanes, everywhere. Some of them succumbed at once; others lingered on for days. Some women and girls of great vitality fought it off for weeks, but the end was invariably the same. I myself had attended some hundreds of stricken women, performed dozens of autopsies – these were soon abandoned – but I was still wholly ignorant of the nature of the disease.

It was peculiar to women as haemophilia is peculiar to men, and though a few men were believed to have died of it – I cannot vouch for the truth of this – such cases must have been rare indeed. They could and did carry the disease, but, as a general rule, were themselves immune. It spread from country to country with horrifying swiftness. America, which had warning of its coming, China, Australia, and other countries far from the scene of war, tried to close their stations and airports, but it seemed to be carried on the wind; there was no keeping it out. Women were isolated, sent up in captive balloons, taken to the tops of high mountains, injected with every known serum, but death came to them all. Since the Eight Hours' War they had been perishing in their hundreds of thousands, in their millions, all over the world. The contagion had spread to the most remote islands, to the heart of Africa, to lonely desert places, everywhere. Not one place on the face of the earth was now free from it.

The time was coming, and had, indeed, almost come, when there would not be a woman or a female child left alive.

As soon as this fact had fully penetrated men's minds, great numbers of them chose death in preference to living, bereaved, in a womanless world. Faced with the cheerless prospect of the cessation of all human life, they preferred to follow their mothers, wives, sisters.

Many others went insane. Now and then poor maddened souls would still rush into the street, shrieking out – in biblical language, as a rule – the doom that was upon us all. The authorities dealt promptly with these unfortunates. They were taken away, and, if crazed beyond all cure, put gently and painlessly to sleep.

Some parts of the world were in complete chaos, particularly those Eastern countries which had not yet thrown off the inertia that fatalism brings. There the people had fallen into such apathy that the dead lay in the streets and the living merely awaited their turn to die. But even here the League of Health – offspring of the old League of Nations, which was believed to have outgrown its usefulness – sent medical officers out in planes to shower disinfectants upon the stricken areas, so that the plagues engendered there should spread no further. They were then isolated and abandoned.

But in most other countries a sturdier spirit prevailed. If it were useless to hope, it was equally useless to despair. "Let us at least end like men," Mr. Hardy, our Prime Minister, had besought his countrymen; and President Gildersleeve, in America, had shown the same sanity and fortitude. In both countries the troops (the National Guard) were in command of the essential services, and life was continuing feebly yet without disorder. There being nothing to hope for, there was also nothing to struggle for. Even robbery seemed pointless, for so suddenly and in such proportions had the population decreased that there was food for everyone and work for all those who wished to work. The Government, calculating the nation's resources and the shortness of the time remaining, resolved to live like a spendthrift. There was no need to conserve, no need to look to and think of the future. The food-supply seemed assured. There were fewer suicides among farmers and the producers of the world's food than among any other class of the community. They seemed willing to work on, patiently and faithfully, let the world end when it must.

In the midst of the general grief and horror, England's girl queen, Henrietta, was mourned only as other women were mourned. She had not yet taken a husband, and, when her brief life flickered out, the Palace staff was dismissed and the Palace closed. All that was needed in the way of government was a man who could keep order, so that those who wished to live out their lives in peace could do so. This task Mr. Hardy, with the help of the Ministers and the Commons, seemed quite capable of performing. I had never been a great admirer of Mr. Hardy. He had always seemed to me a hollow, conventional man behind whose somewhat oracular booming lay little real intelligence, but since the beginning of these grim events I have been describing he had shown considerable firmness, foresight, and courage.

The death cars which sped about the city, collecting the bodies of the dead, rushed them to the mouth of the Thames, where they were placed in motor-ships, which took them far out to sea. No other kind of burial was possible, for within a brief time – sixteen days, to be exact – the population had been cut down to something just over a third of its normal size. The bodies were weighted, and the work was done as decently and speedily as might be. Funeral services of any sort were, of course, out of the question, but memorial services were being conducted day and night in all the big churches and cathedrals.

The majority of very young male children were being taken care of in hastily organized institutions, where their fathers had access to them. For these unfortunate infants there was only the mournful prospect of ending their days in a thinly populated and ruined world, and one of their number would someday know himself to be the only human creature left alive on earth. Or so, at any rate, it seemed at this time.

I had no wish to put an end to my own life, but I was thankful, nevertheless, that I was eighty-eight, and unlikely to live more than a few years longer. For I did not, then, propose to continue injecting myself with Evitalin, but meant to grow old and finish as soon as nature would allow me. Future events were to cause me to change my plans, but I will tell you about this in due course.

I was walking down Whitehall because I had just been present at the death-bed of an old friend of my wife's, who lived in one of the big hotels overlooking the Mall. My next appointment was on the landing-ground just beyond the Houses of Parliament.

The old Houses of Parliament had been so badly damaged in the Twenty Days' War of 1950 that they had had to be rebuilt, after ten years of fruitless and dangerous patching-up. They were now unbelievably lovely, being made of chromium steel and greenish glass, and had been designed by the great Canadian architect, Sir Wilfrid Lecomte. The softly suffused daylight of the interior was dimmed by huge modern tapestries, and at night the whole building glowed and reflected itself in the clear waters of the Thames like something seen in a dream. For the Thames was no longer the muddy, unsightly stream it is today. Its bed had been dredged and cleaned; its waters, before they entered the city, were filtered of the mud of the stream higher up, so that they were blue and clear, and hundreds of people swam in them during the summer. All along the smooth and grassy banks ornamental or fruit-bearing trees were planted, and flowers of every sort.

This had been the task of unskilled workers for many years. For unemployment had gone on increasing with the perfecting of machinery and the new air power until finally all those who could not be absorbed by the trades made parks and beautified England instead of living idly and miserably on the dole. Outside the cities – and even these were now wholly without slums or dirt – the countryside was like a great garden and there was not a stretch of ugly, barren highway in the whole land. No flimsy bungalows, knocked together overnight, no little sham-Tudor monstrosities, defaced the rural districts. Skilfully planned centres had been built, surrounded by gardens, and people lived in well-designed communities and had their own theatres (the cinema as we know it today no longer existed, for there was a cinema combined with wireless and television in every home), their own schools, churches, pleasure halls, golf links, and tennis courts. Even the sea coast, once exploited by every builder and land agent until there remained hardly a mile of shore that was not an ugly, untidy litter, was at last reclaimed, and here, too, thoughtful planning provided for rich or poor by building holiday centres that left miles of coast free and open and unspoilt.

In fact, the England in which I was living at eighty-eight was a very lovely place; smokeless, dirtless, bright, and suited to the needs of a proud and progressive race. But, alas! man had failed to root out of his nature national prejudices, factional hatreds, jealousy, cruelty, bigotry. Therefore the race was to end. England had not been wholly blameless. Had she, one of the most influential of the League of English-Speaking Nations, spoken in firmer tones, made clearer her views as to the total illegality of offensive warfare *under any circumstances* whatever, that group of nations which precipitated the Eight Hours' War might have stayed their hands.

But England feared the secession of one of her own States, and, believing that she and the other associated States might be driven to use force to preserve the League, dared not insist on the criminality of force to others.

It is true that the State in question had been provocative in the extreme, but had she been allowed to secede it is more than likely that she would have learnt, soon enough, the disadvantages of being outside the League, and would have asked to be included once more. So, at least, many people believed, but no one had heart any longer for controversy or blame. What was done was done. The human race, so astonishing in its development, so limitless in its ingenuity and in its possibilities, had defeated itself, and must die. After us the infinite night, unless, by other miraculous combination of circumstances, human life might once more evolve and the human voice once more be heard upon earth atter a silence of millions of years.

The tragedy was too vast to be realized. Men's minds recoiled upon themselves. It was almost impossible for the brain to retain the idea that "Finis" had been written across the pages of history. Men stopped each other in the streets and looked wildly into each other's faces. "It's true, I suppose?" they would ask. "I'm not crazy, or dreaming? All this has really happened?"

The streets at this time were paved with thick and immensely hard-wearing blocks of rubber, coloured green. The pavements, raised a good two and a half feet above the streets, were of the same material, and I can recall, as I write, the pleasant springy feeling of them under my feet. There were no longer any narrow streets, most of them being as wide, or nearly as wide, as Whitehall, and they were spanned at intervals, by graceful, airy bridges of steel and glass which cast hardly a shadow and over which pedestrians passed in safety. Small trees were planted all along the roads, and the whole scene was extremely bright and colourful. There were still old people – I was not one of them – who lamented the loss of grey or blackened stone, the dirty grey of old pavings – the sooty old London, in fact, that was no more. But the improvement in health, cheerfulness, and general happiness was immeasurable, and I for one would not have gone back to those (these!) old dark days for anything.

This sunny April, flowers were springing up everywhere: under the trees, in window-boxes, along the riverbanks, in the parks. They even decorated the edge of the landing-ground I was approaching – one of the four such landing grounds spanning the Thames between Richmond and the Tower. It was built of steel and concrete but floored with the same green rubber, and was high enough to allow the boats which sped up and down the river to pass underneath. Planes – all helicopters of great lightness and flexibility – were ascending and descending. Only people connected with Government services were allowed to use these landing-grounds. The general public were obliged to use those outside the city, from which fast aerial cable cars conveyed them to their homes. The great freight-carrying planes discharged their loads on special freight-grounds also beyond the city limits, and the goods were rushed to their destination by the underground.

I went to one of the shelters on the field, took up some glasses, and scanned the sky to see if I could pick up Alan Holderness, the young American who was to have married Helen. He was just due, and I presently discovered his machine by the blue circle and the broad red stripe beneath it. I looked upon Alan as a son, and he was the last close link with my family now remaining to me. I hoped he would spend some weeks with me, for my loneliness was becoming a torment.

America had become almost as familiar to English people as their own country. The Atlantic was crossed by hourly services. During the summer holidays England would be half emp tied of its population, for, so cheap was air travel, people flew to Canada, the Rockies, the High Sierras, the Pacific coast as easily as they now travel to Bournemouth or Scarborough.

Helen had loved America, and had flown there a dozen times at least in the last year. She and Alan had met in New York, when they were both attempting record flights into the stratosphere. She went in for this competition without telling me, and it was the one and only occasion on which I was really displeased with her, though I forgave her soon enough.

Alan came down very prettily, but got out of his machine slowly and heavily. A mechanic wheeled it away to its garage, and Alan came towards me looking very tired and utterly hopeless. I knew the errand he had been on, and my heart sank.

"Well," he said, taking my arm, "I've flown from New York to San Francisco, and from Chicago to Texas. There isn't a hope. I've talked to men just back from Maine and Florida, from the Bahamas and the Philippines and the Hawaiian Islands; from China, Russia, India, South America, Africa. It's the same everywhere. They're all dead, dying, or doomed. In India there wasn't one left alive. Not one. They went quickest in the hot countries. I wish to heaven I could go completely crazy. Plenty of my friends have."

He brushed a hand across his forehead. "I feel about halfway there, but it isn't enough."

"It's time for lunch, my dear boy," I said to him. "I'm doing my own cooking now, but Benglass is learning. Anyhow, there's a cold chicken and a salad and a bottle of wine."

"I'm not hungry," he said. "I didn't eat a mouthful yesterday. What's the good?"

"I can't spare you, Alan," I told him. "You're all I have left.

All this seems like an evil dream to me, but still it's a dream of some interest. Stay in it with me."

"If I do," he said with a brief and weary smile, "it'll be for your sake, not to please myself."

"Then please me," I said, "by eating a good lunch."

My flat was high up in a new building overlooking the river. Like the majority of modern buildings, so much of it was of glass that one never felt completely indoors. Broad windows of clear glass commanded a fine stretch of the Thames, on the far side of which were trees just breaking into leaf, and, rising up behind them, delicate, shining towers. I had kept a good deal of my old furniture – Helen and Laura used to laugh at me for my sentimental refusal to part with it – and the big desk in my consulting-room was the very one I am now writing on. The stuffs were mostly of light woods in natural tones or in white, but the tapestries – there had been a great revival in tapestry-weaving – were in gay, bright colours, and depicted scenes of the past. On the table in the living-room were coloured photographs (coloured, of course, by the new process) of my wife and of Helen and Laura, and Alan picked them up, looked at them without a word, and put them down again.

He stayed with me for two weeks. During that time the few women reported as still remaining alive had succumbed to the plague. I well remember going with Alan one day into one of the many sound-proof listening-rooms that were dotted about the streets and parks, and hearing the announcer say that a woman still lived in the mountains of Bulgaria, a child continued to breathe in Manitoba, and a girl had been found dying but not yet dead in a village in Central America. We waited for half an hour or so listening to a talk on housekeeping, and presently the same announcer told us, in a voice which he tried to keep as matter-of-fact as possible, that the old woman and the girl had now died, but that the child was still breathing.

"So far as is known," he said, "this two-year-old girl is the last survivor of the female sex remaining upon earth." There was a five minutes' interval during which a Chopin Nocturne was played, and then the voice spoke again. "We regret to announce that the child, which a few moments ago was lying gravely ill in Manitoba, has now died." What more he said we couldn't hear, for just then a man went mad and rushed screaming horribly out of the listening-room. Alan and I presently went out, for the faces of the men sitting there were not pleasant to see. They sat with bent heads, their hands hanging between their knees, like men under sentence of death. We walked slowly back to my flat without speaking.

That night there was a wireless proclamation by Mr. Hardy, the Prime Minister. He implored his fellow-countrymen to continue to live like decent, God-fearing citizens. There was work for everyone, he said, food for everyone; life could still be lived bravely and finely. "Let us go down with the ship," he said, "with bands playing and flags flying." He went on to say that international games and sports were being organized for young men, and contests of every description. It must be remembered, he told us that night, that the future of the world was never more, at any time, than an *idea* in our minds. None of us could hope to have any share in it except through our children, and even there the hope was illusory and sentimental. Now, except for the loss of our dear ones, we were little worse off than our short-lived ancestors, who, *had they but known,* were also living in a doomed world.

This talk had the effect of infuriating Alan.

"Doomed?" he cried. "Who doomed it, I'd like to know? Old dunderheads like Hardy himself. Why doesn't he speak out for once, and tell the truth? The human race has been a ghastly, absurd failure. It's nothing but a monstrous joke. It took several million years for it to evolve out of the slime. And it evolved for what? For what? To commit suicide. Funny, isn't it? It makes me laugh all right. If I once got really started, I don't believe I'd ever stop laughing." He began to walk up and down excitedly. He looked ill and haggard, and I was very anxious about him.

"You'd think some of our sages might have seen this coming," he went on. "It was predicted a long time ago. Who takes up the sword shall perish by the sword. Those who drop the gas bomb shall perish by the gas bomb. Blood that is spilt cries out for more blood to avenge it. We've made property sacred enough, but not life; not that mysterious spark. A man who steals is a social outlaw. A man who robs others of that sacred spark is a hero if he chooses his time well. A world so crazy deserves to end. I'm glad it's ending. Yes, I'm glad, glad!"

At last I persuaded him to drink a glass of Euthanol and go to bed. This was the discovery of a Swedish scientist named

Larssen and was one of the greatest boons ever given to mankind. It could not be taken with suicidal intent, as too much of it produced immediate sickness and vomiting. Taken in moderate quantities it gave a most refreshing and healing sleep, and at the same time stimulated the recuperative powers. For those suffering from mental shock or in great physical pain it was a godsend, for though the sleeper was totally unconscious as far as bodily sensation or thought were concerned, he preserved a sort of time sense, and on waking was aware of the lapse of hours or days. This knowledge of intervening time was especially helpful in cases of bereavement and mental suffering, and without it would not have been nearly so efficacious.

When Alan woke, thirty-six hours later, he was much more cheerful and his nerves were soothed and calmed. He talked of joining in the world-wide search that was being organized in most countries for a living woman, and although I believed the search to be wholly useless, and its only object to provide many thousands of depressed young men with an occupation, I thought it best not to try to dissuade him. He was gone for about ten days, and by the time he returned all hope had vanished.

I saw my patients at my usual hours, and Alan spent a good deal of his time quietly reading indoors. My heart ached for him. He was a splendid specimen of a young man, as Helen was of a young woman. What might not their children have been, and their children's children? What might not the world have been but for the murder in the hearts of fools?

Men came to consult me with an apologetic air.

"I know it's ridiculous, doctor, to want to live at all, but suicide is against my principles and I may as well keep as fit as I can. I've still got my golf, and sometimes my friends come in for a rubber of bridge, and lately I've taken up amateur theatricals. On the whole, life is just bearable."

Most of them talked in some such fashion. One old retired admiral told me he'd never been so happy in his life. I had met his wife and daughters, and the remark was, perhaps, not as brutal as it sounds. But for the most part men lived dully and half-heartedly, merely existing from day to day. All zest for life had gone; pulses were slow and heavy, hearts enfeebled. I did what I could for them and was glad of the work, for it kept me busy.

Poor Alan had no such occupation to keep him from thinking. His father was the famous Philadelphia gynaecologist, Dr. Bertram Holderness, to whom we owe much of our knowledge of sex-control. In 1958 he began putting his theories into practice, and within the next ten years had so perfected them that *Sex At Choice* became common knowledge. It soon became the custom for all young parents to see that their first child was a boy. (I was perfectly well acquainted with the methods employed, and yet now, tonight, as I write this account, I find my memory already growing hazy. I have made some notes, and they are here on my desk beside me, but they hardly seem to me to make sense. Is there some important thing that I have already forgotten? If that is the case, I must hurry on with this story, or more of it may escape me than I thought possible.)

As soon as the disease began to spread, Alan had offered himself and his fast new plane to the Government. He was asked to fly to Japan to bring back a new serum which seemed, for a while, to be stemming the tide of death. He did so in record time, but its effects were only temporary and its use soon abandoned. But for that he would have been with Helen when she died.

Then the amazing thing happened.

One day – it was the second Monday in May – Alan flew to Scotland to see a friend, promising to be back within the next twenty-four hours. I saw my patients as usual, and when the last one had gone I took my hat and went for a stroll, as it was a particularly warm, bright day. The sun sparkled on domes and towers of delicately coloured glass – forget the glass of the Crystal Palace or any glass buildings you have ever seen, for this was something quite different – and the whole effect was one of great lightness, transparency, and iridescence. The wonder was that anything could look so delicate – with a sort of soap-bubble delicacy – and yet be so enduring. The young leaves were vividly green; the flowers, untouched by soot or smoke, starred the bright grass; the sky was as clear and blue as the sky that roofs an idle summer sea. Man had come very near to making himself a paradise, I thought, and now must leave it to silence and decay. Not a soul alive this lovely day but must wish with his whole heart and soul that time could be turned backward and the world be given another chance. And if it were given another chance? The lesson, probably, would still have been unlearnt.

Imperfect, insufficient love digs its own inevitable grave. In the faulty heart of man is the seed of his own destruction.

I particularly noticed that day the spurious air of bustle caused by the gradual demolition of unwanted buildings. The authorities had calculated the number of homes and offices that would be needed for the accommodation of the present population, and those that were superfluous were being destroyed. They were bound to fall into disrepair in time, and endanger life; besides, the spectacle of empty, uncared-for buildings would be very depressing. It was not the intention of the Government that the dwindling citizens should be compelled to end their days dismally among ruins, and a programme of increasing destruction was being planned. All this kept many thousands of workers employed, for there was, of course, no new building of any sort going forward. The first to go were the shops that had catered for women. They were soon done away with, the ground levelled, and grass and trees planted in the open spaces. A number of theatres were left, for men were turning more and more to the stage, and plays of surprising skill and interest were being written by companies of amateurs who hoped in this way to maintain their sanity and their interest in life.

At the end of an hour's stroll I returned to my flat, and saw in the main doorway of the building a small, ragged boy of ten or eleven. He was examining the list of the flats' tenants, and the doorkeeper, with the indifference that now characterized the average person's behaviour, had not troubled to find out what the child wanted, but was leaning against a small tree at the edge of the pavement watching a hovering helicopter, which, like a silver hawk, was awaiting its turn to come down upon the landing-ground.

I asked the boy if he were looking for someone, and to my surprise he spoke my name. The authorities were doing what they could for these motherless children, but many of them contrived to run practically wild. This boy looked thoroughly neglected. He was dirty and his hair was unbrushed, but he had a frank, intelligent little face and a well-shaped head. He spoke well and politely.

"Please, sir, I want Dr. Selwyn," he said.

When I told him that I was Dr. Selwyn, he slipped his hand into mine and drew me further into the hall. When he was quite certain we were out of the doorkeeper's hearing he looked up into my face with an air of great secrecy and importance and whispered:

"Where's your black bag?"

I explained that it was upstairs.

"What is it, my boy?" I asked. "Is someone ill?"

He looked round him, to be sure no one was near, and then, raising himself on the toes of a pair of shabby shoes, whispered:

"It's Auntie Stella."

I felt a sort of freezing in my blood. My heart gave a great leap and I held tightly to the boy's arm, for the world seemed to be slipping from me. In a second or two I was myself again, and ready to laugh at the way I had almost allowed myself to be hoaxed. This, I thought, was precisely the sort of practical joke a neglected small boy would be apt to play, and I accepted it as a joke and forgave him.

"Come up to my flat with me," I said, "and then we can talk."

And it struck me that had this been a practical joke, my invitation, spoken in a rather stern voice, might have frightened him. But he followed me very willingly, and, when the lift took us to my floor, he showed no disposition whatever to escape. I took him into my consulting-room.

"Now," I said, frowning at him, "what's this about an Aunt Stella? Come, tell me the truth, boy, tell me the truth."

"She's in our house," he said, looking at me with candid eyes. "She won't wake up. She just sleeps and sleeps."

However unbelievable, this seemed honest enough.

"Are you sure she's asleep? Would you know if she were dead?"

"I know when people are dead," he said, nodding his head emphatically. "I saw mum when she was dead, and my sister Lucy, and my Auntie May. But Auntie Stella isn't dead. She's just asleep. I can't wake her up."

"What made you come to me?"

"Because a boy I know knows Mr. Benglass, your chauffeur. And one day when we were walking past here he said, 'That's where Mr. Benglass's old doctor lives.'"

I was beginning to feel that this thing might be true. But, even if it weren't true, I had time on my hands and I could stand being hoaxed as well as the next person. So I hesitated no longer, but picked up my bag and we went down in the lift. I told the idle doorkeeper to call me a taxi, for I thought it best not to let Benglass know where I was going.

The doorkeeper took a key out of his pocket, opened a box by the front door, and turned a handle sharply. In a minute a taxi was there, summoned from a rank in front of Parliament. The boy gave the address, which was across the river, and we got in. All traffic now went in one direction only, moving very rapidly along a series of loops. The intersecting streets crossed each other at different levels, so that cars moving in one direction passed through short tunnels underneath, and those moving in the opposite direction passed overhead. It made one's journeys somewhat roundabout, but at least one could travel at high speed and without stops.

For the last three years not a single pedestrian had lost his life in the streets of London. We crossed the river by one of the new glass and steel bridges – a lovely thing – and presently found ourselves in a district of small and shabby houses. Few of these remained, either having been destroyed in the Twenty Days' War or pulled down and rebuilt. The people who lived in them were old-fashioned folk who clung to their homes stubbornly rather than move to the airy, light, convenient flats which had been built in great numbers.

We drew up before a dingy little house that had probably been built about seventy years earlier. Its windows were small; its hall, I knew, narrow and dark. I dismissed the taxi on hearing that there was a rank not far away, the boy opened the door, and we went in.

It was just such a house as I myself had lived in as a boy – stuffy, insanitary and inconvenient. The stairs rose straight out of the cramped front hall, and they had not had a broom on them for some time. I followed the boy to the floor above, and, with feelings that I can leave to your imagination, watched him open the door of the front bedroom. Then I stepped inside.

There was a young woman lying in bed, and she was no more dead than I was.

She was, I guessed, between twenty-two and three, and looked perfectly healthy. Her sleep had every indication of being a Euthanol sleep, and, bending over her, I detected the pleasant, herb-like odour of Euthanol on her breath.

She lay very straight in the bed, her arms crossed on her breast almost as if she had disposed herself so for her coffin. Between the fingers of one hand was a tightly folded piece of paper with writing on it.

"That's about me," said the boy, nodding towards it. Once having got me there, he had quite lost his air of grave responsibility and now climbed on the footboard of the bed and balanced himself on his stomach across it. I persuaded him to stand quietly on his feet.

"Tell me if you can," I said, "when she fell asleep. How many days ago was it? Was it yesterday?"

"No, not yesterday. And not the day before." He kept track of the days by the meals he had had, it appeared. "Yesterday I ate with Billy Gorman and his father. And the day before that I had dinner with the milkman. And the day before that, I think, a soldier took me to a place and gave me some dinner. Maybe it was that day, or maybe the day before. I don't really remember."

"Was she quite well," I asked, "when she fell asleep?"

He shook his head. She had had a pain here, he said, putting his hands to his temples. She had kissed him and said that she was going to die, and that he must be a good boy and go to his uncle in Mitcham. But she hadn't died and so he'd stayed on, partly because he didn't like his uncle much and partly because he didn't want to leave his Aunt Stella.

I told him that his aunt was not going to die. I gave him some money and told him to go out and buy some milk and buns and fruit and bring them back.

"I'm going to stay here until your aunt wakes up. And don't say a word about this to anyone, do you understand? Not one word."

He told me, with pride, that he'd promised his Aunt Stella not to tell anyone about her, and that he'd kept his word until the time came when he had thought he had better come and tell me. I praised him for his good sense and sent him out. I then made a thorough examination of the sleeping girl.

She was perfectly well, perfectly normal. She had no trace whatever of the plague that had destroyed all other women. How she had escaped it was a complete mystery. I took the paper from her fingers, hoping to find the explanation, but she had not chosen to give it. The writing was neat, firm, and full of character. I cannot of course remember the exact words, but roughly it was as follows:

"I want whoever finds me to take great care of Freddie, my nephew, if he is still here. He is a very good boy, and I have told him to go to his uncle at No. 40 Perthshire Mansions, Mitcham, but he may not wish to leave me until he must. I have been perfectly well until today, May 8th. I believe I have survived all the other women in the world. At least, I heard it announced on the wireless that all hope of finding a living woman was now abandoned. Why I have been able to fight off death for so long doesn't matter now, for I believe it is on me at last. I'm a coward, and, besides, I don't want Freddie to see me die. He has seen enough of death. So I am taking a glass of Euthanol and hope to die in my sleep. I haven't been out of this house for weeks, because wherever I went lately, people have followed me, staring at me and expecting to see me collapse and be taken away. Some men came into the house last week, searching for a living woman, but I hid in a small cupboard and they didn't find me. The pain in my head is very bad, and now I am going to drink the Euthanol and sleep until the end comes. Life has not been kind and I've had little happiness here. That there should still be wars is a disgrace to humanity, for there is unavoidable sorrow and trouble enough, heaven knows, without them. War belongs to the dark ages, but has been fostered until our own day by men who saw no other way of getting money, advancement, or glory. Men! Without them, how happy we could have been! We ought to have destroyed the majority of them years ago, only keeping enough to increase the population, or perhaps keep it from declining. They've made such an atrocious muddle of things that they deserved to die (and they will!), but it's we who must die first. Some man will find this letter. I want him to know that with my last breath I cursed him and all his kind.

"STELLA MORROW"

I read this sitting beside the bed. A young woman of strong character and sound views, I thought. But these facts were written, clearly enough, in her face. Let me try to describe her.

She had no beauty. Lest admirers of the sickly, calculated, unreal charms of our film stars imagine that some such girl lay here, let me assure them that no film company would have dreamt of choosing her for the heroine of such a tale as this. Her features were irregular. Her lips were full, I might almost say coarse, though far from coarse in expression. Her nose was short and blunt, her eyes small and deeply set. She had a full and intelligent forehead and a firm and slightly prognathous jaw. She was of medium height and weight – I judged the former to be about five foot five or six and the latter to be in the neighbourhood of nine and a half stone. Her wrists and ankles were strong; some people might have thought them thick, but they were by no means unsightly. (When I see a woman walking on pipe-stems a shudder goes through me.) Her skin was beautifully clear, and even now the blood showed in her cheeks. Her hair was a very light brown, and inclined to curl about the forehead. She had scarcely any eyebrows at all. Eyebrows don't suit everybody, and they wouldn't have suited her. I parted her lips and saw strong teeth, as white as a young dog's. Lifting an eyelid, I saw that her eyes were blue. Very English, that small blue eye and thick eyelid. Very Saxon, I ought to say. Civilization had affected her little, I thought. Such girls have made hay in fields and made love in lanes since long before the coming of the Normans. She looked like the daughter of plain farming folk, and yet I knew, without looking at the letter, that she had been quite well educated. (It was difficult to avoid a good education in 1985.) She would have, I thought, a good deal of shrewdness, a good deal of common sense. In my opinion there is no common sense equal to that of a really sensible woman. There was a great deal of truth in what she had written. With men well in the minority, with women the dominant sex, yet with enough men among them to ensure the continuation of the race as well as to lead the way intellectually (but without the mischievous power to destroy the works of their own hands), what a world women might have made! Evolution, though slower, would have been far more sure. But of course it could never have happened. Men would never have taught them how to choose the sex of their children, and they would have been too tender-hearted to deny life to their male children, once they were born. They would have cared for them in secret, and men would soon have become sufficiently numerous to begin making wars and trouble again.

I sat with my fingers on the pulse of this historic, this very literally epoch-making girl. I believed that I felt the pulse-beats of a new world. The blood that moved in these veins would flow through the veins of the New Men as they sat in some small lonely settlement surrounded by crowding forests of young trees. For the trees would conquer England again as they would conquer all but the prairies and desert places of the world, until men grew numerous enough to hack their way into the open once more, and plan and build anew.

The boy returned, and we sat eating buns and fruit and drinking milk. I warmed some milk for the girl, for when people wake after a long Euthanol sleep they wake hungry, and I thought that she must wake soon.

It was after seven when she opened her eyes. The lowering sun was shining through the curtains, which I, like a conspirator, had closely drawn, and the sparrows were twittering noisily outside. I heard a change in her breathing. Presently she gave several long sighs, stretched herself, turned on her side, and yawned widely. Quite suddenly, her eyes flew open. She was asleep; then, between two ticks of a clock, she was awake and looking at me.

She knew, from the touch of my fingers on her pulse, that I was a doctor, and showed neither surprise nor alarm. Her pulse remained quite steady, quite normal. She rolled her head on the pillow and saw Freddie, who, excited by the signs of waking, had taken up his favourite position, balancing himself on his stomach across the footboard of the bed. Her first words were:

"Get down, Freddie dear. You know you scratch the woodwork with your shoes." Then she turned back to me again.

"I ought to be dead, by rights," she said.

I patted her hand. "You're not going to die. You're perfectly well. Now you must eat and drink a little."

"Did Freddie fetch you?" she asked.

I told her how we had found each other.

"That was clever of you, Freddie," she said. "But you know you ought to have gone to your uncle's, as I told you to."

"Not while you weren't dead, Auntie Stella," he protested.

I told her I thought the boy had done perfectly right and had shown himself to be discreet and resourceful.

She wanted to know how he had got his food, and he told her.

She lowered her eyes, looking ashamed.

"You must think me an awful coward, doctor," she said, "but I was certain I was going to die, and I wanted to die tidily, here in this bed. Do you blame me very much?"

I told her I would probably have done the same in her place. It was, in fact, what millions of other women had done. The manufacturers of Euthanol must have made a colossal fortune – and much good it would do them! She sat propped up against her pillows drinking her milk and eating some buns. The room was warm, and she pushed away the bedclothes. She was wearing pale blue artificial silk pyjamas, the sort that girls buy ready-made, I think, and she had embroidered her initials on the pocket in a darker blue. I was longing to ask her to what miraculous cause she owed her life, but waited until I could talk to her alone. When she had eaten and drunk, I asked Freddie to go downstairs.

"But don't go away," his aunt said, "because I shall want you to do some errands for me soon. You'll have to go out and buy something for supper. I shan't dare to go out myself."

I told them both that on no account must anyone know what we knew, and said that I would discuss my plans for them later. When Freddie had gone she said:

"I suppose I'm the only one left?"

I nodded, without speaking.

"And I suppose you want to know how and why I'm here at all?" She didn't wait for me to answer, but said, "Have you ever heard of a man named Gordon Hummel? Dr. Gordon Hummel?"

"Never," I told her.

"You wouldn't, I suppose. He wasn't qualified. I expect you'd call him a quack. But I'd better begin from the beginning."

I'm not going to attempt to tell her story in her own words. I can remember conversations pretty accurately, but to try to repeat, word for word, what she told me would be absurd. I will tell you the facts in my own way. She had a pleasing voice, firm and clear, and she spoke with very few corrections, hesitations, or repetitions. I saw that she had an orderly mind – *beaucoup de suivre*, as the French say, in her ideas. I had not overestimated her good sense.

(Why, oh, why, did women not make use of their collective good sense to prevent wars? Why did they never organize? Women are the world's true internationals. Their lack of national prejudice, their adaptability, their mental fluidity, all fit them for this role. Why did they never play it? Why did they never assert themselves in any ways that mattered? Why did they never find, never even seek, solidarity? The power they might have had! That was what Helen meant when she uttered those dying words: "We deserve this. We might have prevented it and we didn't. We deserve to die.")

She was born near Stroud, in Gloucestershire. (About this I shall have something to say at the end of my story.) Her grandparents were hard-working farming people, who had, of course, owned their own farm until the Communist Government that followed the war, and lasted from 1951 to 1967, made all farming collective. With the return of the Reactionaries, collective farming ceased and their farm was given back to them in their old age. By this time they had got used to the other way of things, and were glad to hand over their responsibilities to their son and daughter-in-law, this girl's parents. Stella went to a good local school, where she got on well, showing a special aptitude for games and physical training. When she was seventeen she made up her mind to be games mistress at a girls' school, and at eighteen such a post was found for her near London. So she came to London, and was offered a room in the home of her sister-in-law, Mrs. Longstreet, whose son Freddie was. An aerial car took her to and from the school daily. I gathered that she was very popular there, and loved her work. Then, one unhappy day, she fell in love.

She didn't mince words or try to conceal from me what she felt for this man. The calm, sensible, matter-of-fact girl lost her head completely, and loved with a blindness and abandon rare in these days of sexual tolerance, sexual freedom and enlightenment. (From the age of ten years, every child was now fully instructed concerning the facts of life and the relations between the sexes. Mystery there was none, or, if there were, it was the same mystery that surrounds all the phenomena of life. There was nothing sly, nothing morbid, nothing concealed. To steal the happiness of another, the welfare of another, by a thoughtless, selfish, impulsive act was a serious matter, and the perpetrator was soon made to feel his responsibility and the anti-social nature of his – or her – behaviour. Public opinion was a powerful deterrent, for what the last thirty years had done was to weaken selfish individualism and to strengthen the collective spirit.)

The young man was an engineer of great promise. He was clever, good-looking, and unscrupulous. He didn't scruple, at least, to accept this ardent girl's complete devotion, to promise marriage as soon as his financial position was sufficiently sound, and then to throw her over when that time came for a lovely young actress who was her opposite in every way.

His name was Ansel Rainier, and he was employed by the firm of Kasha & Bird, the makers of helicopters and air liners. In his spare time he had been working on a design for a new type of dirigible rocket car. This he perfected, and when he circled the Earth in seven hours, he became famous overnight.

When Stella first fell in love with him, and – or, so she was led to believe – he with her, he was merely an ambitious young nobody who was not at all averse to accepting the adoration of the nineteen-year-old games mistress who believed in, encouraged, and worshipped him with all her heart. When fame came to him, he married the actress without a word of warning. She was well known, and extremely beautiful. The shock almost drove Stella mad. She threw up her job – everyone at the school knew of her love-affair, and her humiliation was more than she could bear –and shut herself in her sister-in-law's house. She wanted only to keep out of people's way and lick her wounds in private, but Mrs. Longstreet, fearing that she might kill herself, called in a quack doctor of her acquaintance named Hummel, who was lodging in a house nearby.

That Hummel, the quack, was a genius of the first order, is clear. He was born in Frankfurt of a German father and a Scottish mother, and came of a long line of doctors and scientists. Since his sixteenth year he had thought of nothing but of discovering some means by which human beings might be made impervious to all diseases. He believed there might be a way of immunizing the body through the chromosomes. He specialized in experimental cytology, and for twenty-five years had been working on a prophylactic dye or stain, which, made to permeate the body by means of a ray, caused every cell and segment of it to resist the invasion of dangerous germs and poisons. This, at any rate, was Stella's account of it, though precisely what the stain was she didn't know.

Hummel, she said, had experimented on guinea pigs, rabbits, horses, dogs, apes, rats, and mice, but never, as yet, on a human being. He was now ready to do so. (He feared to experiment on himself, lest he should incapacitate himself for further work and so lose, to the race, a discovery of incalculable value.) Finding Stella in a state of complete despair, he told her of his work, hoping to interest her and take her mind off her troubles.

But as soon as she heard of the stain she at once offered herself for his first hu man experiment. “Though in my opinion,” she told him, “you would be doing far more for the happiness of the human race if you could make them immune to love.”

He tried, in his gentle, earnest way, she said, to dissuade her, but she had made up her mind. At last he took her to his laboratory, which was in a disused garage in a nearby street, and there she insisted on undergoing the treatment. She was first given a bath in the dye – a brilliant red colour – and was then subjected for over two hours to a light-bath in a powerful ray of Hummel's own discovery.

At the end of that time her body had entirely absorbed the stain, and her skin had become its normal colour again. She said that she felt dizzy for a little while, but apart from that she felt no ill effects whatever.

After an interval of two weeks, during which she was constantly under Hummel's observation, he injected her with one sort of bacillus after another, with suitable intervals after each injection. None of them had the smallest effect on her. The whole experiment interested her keenly, and for a while she almost forgot her misery. They continued the tests from September until the beginning of March, when Hummel obtained from China some cholera germs of a particularly virulent type. While he was injecting her he somehow let fall the tiny tube and broke it. He at once subjected himself to his own treatment, but it was too late. He sickened, was rushed to an isolation hospital, and there died, after making a desperate fight for life.

His notes were so illegible and his papers were in such disorder that the scientists who later examined them could make little of them. The story created a considerable stir; then the Eight Hours' War came, with its terrible after math, and the matter was forgotten by everyone but Stella herself.

That she could withstand even the unknown death she did not believe. She thought the end merely postponed for a while, and when the pains in her head began – caused, I imagine, merely by lack of fresh air and exercise – she fully believed that death was near.

You can imagine, perhaps, the excitement I felt at hearing her story. In the first place she was, by nature, a very healthy girl. Her chances of reaching old age were unusually good, and her youth could be prolonged, if need be, by Evitalin. In addition to this, she was immune, thanks to Hummel, to all diseases. In fact, nothing short of violence or an accident would be likely to kill her. She was born to be the mother of many children; her broad hips, full bosom, and calm looks suggested great fertility. Did she realize, I wondered, that in her lay all the hope of the future? But I had no mind to speak to her of such matters yet. The thing that most concerned me now was her safety. She must be made safe from discovery, safe from the feverish, the perhaps destructive curiosity of mobs. I made up my mind to take both her and Freddie back with me that night.

She said she would be glad enough to go. She had suffered too much in that house, and would be thankful to see the last of it. She was as anxious not to be seen as I was to keep her hidden.

She told me that packed away in the attic was a suit of men's clothes which she had worn when playing male parts in school theatricals. I told her to put them on, as they would make the journey from the house to my flat considerably safer.

Dressed in coat and trousers, she looked boyish enough to pass muster in the dark, but she was of far too feminine a build to deceive anyone by day. I saw that I would have to keep her carefully hidden until it was decided what should be done with her, a decision that I felt should be in the hands of Mr. Hardy and the Cabinet.

She prepared a very good supper for us. There was a moment of alarm when the post man knocked, bringing a letter for Freddie from his uncle in Mitcham. Unable to get any answer on the telephone, he wrote, he proposed calling at the house and taking his nephew back with him. He had been unable to come before, owing to a bad attack of lumbago and having to do all his own work. He upbraided Freddie for not having been dutiful enough to come to him.

As neither Freddie nor Stella appeared to have much affection for this man, who, they told me, was bad-tempered and very selfish, I advised an immediate departure, and told Freddie to leave a note for him saying that he had been adopted by friends and would be well taken care of.

We left the house just as it was, without turning a key, and, carrying two suitcases, got into a taxi and drove straight to my flat. The bright lights at the entrance gave me some anxious moments, but the doorkeeper was too stupid a fellow to notice much, and barely glanced at my two guests. I gave Stella Helen's room, and put Freddie in Laura's. Alan was occupying the room that had belonged to my wife. I was so disturbed and excited that night that I could hardly sleep, and, in fact, did not close my eyes until I had measured myself out a small dose of Euthanol and drunk it.

When Benglass called me the next morning I told him that I had brought home an orphan boy of ten and his elder brother, who was ill and must not be disturbed. It wasn't the first time I had introduced stray unfortunates into my home, and Benglass showed neither surprise nor curiosity. Before either of my guests were awake – I let them sleep till eleven – I rang up the Prime Minister's secretary and made an appointment with Mr. Hardy for three-thirty that afternoon. I sent Freddie out with Benglass after lunch to buy some new clothes, and advised Stella to stay quietly reading in her room under lock and key, as I knew she would be safer there than anywhere.

Mr. Hardy had married for the second time about six months before the launching of the Eight Hours' War. His wife was a brilliant and charming woman, and had for some years been his private secretary. It was sometimes suggested – and I think rightly – that she was the better Prime Minister of the two. I was touched, that afternoon, by his tragic looks, which contrasted so strongly with the encouraging and undaunted spirit of the talks he had been broadcasting each day. He was, in fact, a broken, afflicted man. His eyes were dull, his manner lifeless; he was suffering from the universal nostalgia and depression, and I couldn't help admiring him for the brave front with which he faced and deceived the world.

As he shook my hand, he said:

"I don't know what you have come to see me about, doctor, but your errand is very timely. Afterwards I'd like to consult you about myself. The fact is that each morning it grows increasingly difficult for me to make up my mind to get out of bed. I'm in constant dread of a breakdown of the will, a nervous collapse. I oughtn't to be here at all. The country needs a younger man."

"Perhaps when I've told you my errand," I said, "you'll feel a younger man."

I made the story as brief as I could, giving him only the essential facts. The effect on him was instantaneous, extraordinary. It brought home to me as nothing else could have done man's mystical dependence on a future, on a belief in a future. We live partly in the past, much in the present, but far more than we realize in a future in which we well know we will take no part whatever. But cut us off from it, and we bleed, we bleed, fatally; the whole being receives a mortal hurt from this amputation. For in some psychic way we draw nourishment from the time to come; we feel ourselves to be part of a great movement, a great growing, a great becoming, which, though unseen, yet surrounds us and is of us, giving life to our impulses, feeding and completing us. Millions have died for this invisible thing; every one of us, in some degree, works and plans and struggles for it, whether we know it or not. It is the love and inspiration, the true mistress of every scientist, every artist. It is dearer and closer to us than now, for with every breath we draw we take in the air of this necessary country, this hopeful horizon land. Indeed, all the world was now suffering from a kind of spiritual claustrophobia, since this life-giving atmosphere was no longer passing into our lungs.

You yourself know what you have felt when scientists have told you how the sun is dissipating its heat; how the time must come, eons from now, when the world will grow cold and dark, and life will vanish from it. You know how cheated you have felt; how your mind has refused to accept, wholly, such a doctrine of futility and despair. Though that time is immeasurably far away, almost beyond thought, we do not choose to believe that the story ends thus, instinctive and indomitable optimists that we are. Imagine, then, the feelings of men who were living in the time I write of, men who were faced with this ending, this closing-down, almost within their own brief lives. You will understand, perhaps, something of what Mr. Hardy felt when he heard of the survival of this infinitesimal life-spark. I saw hope flow back into him again; I watched it lift him up, as the returning tide lifts the once more buoyant hull from the mud where it has lain. His eyes moistened; tears came into them. They loosened, I saw, something that had been frozen in him. He turned away, broke down and sobbed, his face hidden in his hands. Wiping my own eyes, I walked about the room, pretending to look at some prints of the London of my boyhood. Presently he apologized for his weakness, and we smiled at each other and put our handkerchiefs away. He pressed a bell, and, when a servant came, he ordered a half-bottle of champagne.

"Am I a sentimental old fool?" he asked me. "I can't help it if I am."

When we were alone again, we filled our glasses and raised them. With trembling lips Mr. Hardy whispered:

"The Queen, God bless her!"

We drained our glasses, and, like a couple of impetuous boys, flung them into the grate and then clasped hands.

"We'll fetch her to the Palace tonight," he said, in a low voice. "At the same time, I'll order the troops to surround it. Tomorrow morning we'll make our proclamation. It will be the greatest moment in history; yes, in all history. All the bells shall be rung. There'll be thanksgiving services in the churches. You were perfectly right, doctor; I feel a new man. That England should be granted this inestimable blessing! I pray we may prove worthy of it and of *her*."

He rang the bell again and sent for his hat and umbrella.

"I want to pay my respects to her at once," he said.

His excitement, I could see, was growing. From a state of extreme depression he was fast reaching one of almost fanatical exaltation. So sudden was the change that I felt a little concerned for him, and begged him to let me write out a soothing prescription, a suggestion which he brushed aside with impatience.

"No, no, I'm perfectly all right, perfectly. Come along. There's no time to be lost. And I don't like the idea of her being there quite alone."

I said, as we got into his car:

"I hope she'll see eye to eye with us. She's a young woman of surprisingly strong views and character. I'm not sure I oughtn't to see her first, to prepare her a little for what's in store for her."

"But surely, my dear doctor," said Mr. Hardy, "she'll be expecting it. Why, what else could she expect?"

I made no reply to this. I thought it best to let Stella speak for herself.

So little interest was there nowadays in the affairs of the Government that the Prime Minister's goings and comings did not attract the attention of a single citizen. No one saw us leave Downing Street and no one would have stopped to stare if they had. On arriving at the flat, I asked Mr. Hardy to wait for me in the library, and went to speak to Stella. Hearing my voice, she opened the door, and I saw that she had been lying on the bed working out a chess problem.

"Hello," she said. "You haven't been gone long. May I come out now?"

I told her the Prime Minister had come to offer her his congratulations. She looked closely at me.

"What have you been up to?" she asked. But she put a comb through her hair, straightened her tie, and came docilely enough. Though she made me think a little of the principal boys of my early pantomime days, she was completely unselfconscious, and walked into the library without a trace of shyness.

Mr. Hardy had taken up his position between the two big windows and facing the door. I knew he would. As she came in, he advanced a few steps to meet her, and, falling abruptly on one knee, took her hand and kissed it.

"Ma'am," he said, in a voice he could barely control, "I, your humble Prime Minister, give thanks to God for your miraculous preservation. Tomorrow the whole world will give thanks. Long, long may you reign over us, and may we prove ourselves worthy of you. God bless you, ma'am! God bless you!"

She withdrew her hand abruptly and stepped back. She looked affronted and angry, and yet half amused. Before I could speak she burst out:

"What nonsense! I'm not a Queen. I've no intention of becoming a Queen. What on earth's the good of all this make-believe?"

"I think myself you ought to have had a little warning," I said, "but Mr. Hardy felt, and perhaps rightly, that there was no time to be lost. Now let's all sit down and discuss things quietly and sensibly."

"Let me explain the situation, ma'am," began Mr. Hardy, but she interrupted him.

"There's no need to explain anything. It's quite obvious what you expect of me, and I won't have anything to do with it. You got the world into this mess, you men, and you can just stay in it. Why should I have to get you out of it? It's not my doing."

Her eyes sparkled. She put her hands behind her back and looked with indignation from the Prime Minister to me and back again. He now began to perceive the truth of what I had told him – that we had to deal with a very strong-willed young woman. I urged her to sit down, and she did, though on the edge of her chair. We also sat down, on either side of her.

"Ma'am," Mr. Hardy began once more, "the position is this."

"My name is Morrow," she said, "Stella Morrow. I've not been married, so I'm not ma'am or madam. If you want to know the truth, no one would have me."

"What nonsense, my dear," I said. "You're not yet twenty-four. You're a child still."

"Am I?" she cried. "Am I? Don't you believe it, doctor. Don't you believe it, Mr. Prime Minister. There's something hard here" – she struck her breast, over her heart. "Once it was soft, but now it's hard, hard, hard. I'm no child. I've made up my mind about what I want to be and do. I was thinking it over this afternoon, in my bedroom. I mean to live as a man and die as a man. I wasn't wanted as a woman. Why should I be wanted as a Queen? You'd like to make me into a sort of Queen Bee. I know. Well, I won't do it. You can talk till doomsday and I won't change my mind."

Mr. Hardy and I exchanged looks. I guessed that he was deeply perturbed.

"I fear we have broken it to you too suddenly, ma'am," he said. "I should have taken Dr. Selwyn's advice, and let him prepare you for this."

"I'm not a half-wit," she said. "A child of five could grasp the idea. You've been an angel to me, doctor, and I'm sorry I cursed you in my letter, but I'd have stayed where I was if I'd known what you were up to. Why didn't you say to me quite frankly this morning, 'Look here, Stella, you're the only woman there is left, and I think I ought to tell the Prime Minister about you.' Then I'd have expressed my views and we'd have known where we were. Instead of that, you go solemnly off without saying a word to me, and get me all mixed up in this Queen Bee business before I know where I am. Why couldn't you have treated me like a human being?"

"I'm sorry, my dear," I said, and I meant it. "You see, the fact of your existence is the most important fact in the world today, by far. I felt it was a perilous business keeping you here without adequate protection, and so I went and told the head of the Government about it. I wasn't plotting."

"It's just what you were doing, it seems to me," she said. "It's what you men are always doing. Now I'll tell you my own plans for myself. I'm going to live here and keep house for you and do the cooking. I'll only go out at night, if you'd rather. I want a lot of books, and I'd like someone to play chess with. If I can't get anyone else to play with, I'll teach Freddie. I'll be quite content."

I told her it was a wretched life for her. She said she preferred it to any other. She liked me and she wanted to settle down here. Mr. Hardy gave a little cough and said:

"What is your objection, ma'am, to living at the Palace? Surely it's your rightful place? And don't you realize what it would mean to us all? When the doctor told me the wonderful news today, I confess I couldn't restrain my tears."

"I hope you'll forgive me if I say 'Bosh!'" she replied. "Look what you've made of the world. What on earth do you want to go on with the silly business for?"

"Won't you let Mr. Hardy tell you in a few words what he had planned for you?" I asked.

"I can guess what he'd planned." she said, "and really, Mr. Hardy, what's the good? It would just be the same thing over again."

"That," he said, "if I may say so, ma'am, would be up to you. Entirely up to you."

"What do you mean?" she asked. Then, before he could answer, she said, "You mean you'd like me to marry somebody – some healthy specimen, I suppose, whom you'd choose for me –"

"The choice, ma'am, would rest with you." He added, "Within reason, of course."

"Yes, I imagine so. Well, then you'd like me to set to work and produce a large family of girls, and when they'd reached marriageable age you'd expect me to marry them to young men who are now babies and are being cared for in your institutions."

"That is so."

She was silent for a moment.

"It's a sad little world you'd be condemning my children and grandchildren and great-grandchildren to live in, Mr. Prime Minister," she said at last.

"Would you like to live in it yourself?"

"Ma'am," said Mr. Hardy, in his mellowest and best modulated voice, "I have lost my beloved wife, my daughter, and my daughter's daughter. I am old and sad and broken. And yet I would give everything I possess – yes, everything – to live on into this new epoch that it's within your power to create, and watch a world in the making. A world," he said, a little sententiously, I am afraid, "with the dew on it."

Stella sprang up impatiently and went to the window. She turned her back on my view of the Thames, and faced us.

"But the world is always in the making," she said, "and always has been. That's what you rulers and governors have never realized – or never wished to realize. With each new generation you older people could have brought up a new race of men and women, with fresh ideals, higher principles, and an honest desire to remake the world. And it could have been done, too. At any time. But as soon as you saw that desire in the young you just scoffed, and talked about 'older and wiser heads.' You killed our enthusiasms as soon as they were born. You kept power in your own hands until they were too palsied to do anything but cling to the reins. You kept alive in the young all your own hatreds, all your own prejudices. It's the way the old revenge themselves upon the young for being young and inheriting the earth – by saddling their backs with the same old burdens, the same old bitternesses, the same old sorrows and stupidities. A new world, indeed! As if the world wasn't always new, whenever there's a child in a cradle!"

She went abruptly to a table, opened a box, and took out a cigarette. The Prime Minister sprang up to help her, but she had lit it before he reached her. Having made the gesture, he sat down again.

"What you've always done," she went on, "was to send the new world to school to learn all the sins of the old; and, if it refused to conform to your evil old ways, to punish it until it did. Look at your history books. Has there ever been one that began by saying, 'Children, read this and weep! Here is the sad, mad, bad old past, hideous with blood and intolerance and suffering and wrong. Learn from it but one thing – to be different. You will find in it some heroism, some unselfishness, some integrity; more often than not the heroism, unselfishness, and integrity of common men and women. Take what you can find of these, and remember the rest only as a lesson in how not to live, how not to think, how not to die'?"

The Prime Minister made a sound of protest, but she had still more to say.

"Believe me," she went on, "I know. I was a child not long ago myself, and was taught to drink at the same old polluted fountains. And I have worked for four years at a girls' school and watched the same miserable process repeat itself. No, no, Mr. Hardy. A new world wouldn't have suited your books at all. Why, the only man who has ever sincerely wanted to change the world was crucified two thousand years ago, and there has never been another."

There was a moment's silence, and then the Prime Minister said: "It astonishes me, ma'am, to find such pessimism in one so young."

"People who were optimists," she retorted, "must have had their eyes opened these last few months, poor souls."

He had nothing to say to that. He changed the subject.

"Surely you must see, ma'am, that your proper place is at the Palace. You are the only woman in the world..."

"No one's ever said that to me before," she interrupted.

"... and, as such, your welfare is of the utmost value and importance. The doctor agrees with me that you cannot remain here. You would surely be discovered, sooner or later, and then your life would be endangered by brutes or fanatics; you might quite conceivably become the cause of bloodshed and contention. For naturally every country in the world would fight for your possession."

"Really?" she said. "I admit I hadn't thought of that. Dear me, dear me. So you still want to fight, do you, you *men*?"

"I, personally," said the Prime Minister, "do not in theory, and yet I myself, and every man in this country, once the facts are known, would cheerfully lay down his life in your defence."

"But I don't want anyone to lay down his life in my defence," she cried, exasperation in her voice. "And that's why I mean to stay here. Let the world end. Let it end. There's been enough bloodshed."

"Man is a fighting animal," said Mr. Hardy.

"If man is only an animal," she retorted, "then let him give way to other animals more suited to bloody contests. For an animal that will both struggle to inflict pain and death and at the same time struggle to find means to prevent pain and death is too irrational a creature to trouble about. Let's make way for sensible, single-minded lions and tigers and wolves, and have done with it. At least they know what they're about."

She began walking up and down the room, her hands in her pockets. I watched her, growing more and more fascinated by her sound sense and her intelligence.

She had not spoken one word with which I was not, secretly, wholly in agreement.

"In fact, Mr. Prime Minister, those last words of yours have helped me to make up my mind. I admit that for a moment I wavered a little. The idea of bringing up a new race of men gave me a kind of thrill, but it's gone now. For, you see, there'd be bad blood in them; there'd be Cains here and there, in spite of me, and the horrid business would begin all over again. And, really, what's the good? If, after all these millions of years, the best you can say of man is that he's a fighting animal – for you said it with pride, Mr. Prime Minister, you did, I swear you did! – well, if that's the best you can say, then all I can say is, 'Finis!' And the sooner the better. Dig a vast grave for all the men there are left in the world, and erect a towering monument over it, and carve on the monument, 'Man was a fighting animal.' It will look splendid, splendid, when there is no longer a human voice to be heard or a human eye to see!"

The Prime Minister lifted a haggard and whitened face.

"I would like to take back those words, ma'am," he said. "What I should have said is this: that man will always dare to fight for those things he holds most precious."

"I asked you not to call me ma'am," she told him, "and you go on doing it."

He turned to me pleadingly, holding out his hands.

"Dr. Selwyn, can you do nothing, say nothing, that will influence her? I have blundered. I have failed miserably. Be Prime Minister in my place, I implore you. I gladly resign my office. If she refuses to come to the Palace of her own accord, we must take her by force, for her own safety and protection, but that force shall not be directed by me. I shall resign."

"I don't see why," said Stella. "You've been very good in this crisis, I believe – though I won't say you mightn't have done something to avert it – and men still have confidence in you. It's silly to resign because of me. Besides, I think you're only using it as a threat, to bring me to reason. How could Dr. Selwyn be Prime Minister in your place? He's had no training, and he's far too useful where he is. Do let's talk sensibly."

"Then you forbid me to resign?" asked Mr. Hardy.

"Forbid?" she exclaimed. "Of course I don't forbid. I'm not a Queen, and I've no intention of being one."

Her voice had risen a little, and must have been audible from the hall. The door opened slowly, and Alan came into the room. I had forgotten him in the excitement of my discovery, forgotten he had merely flown to Scotland and might return at any moment. And now here he was. Stella, at the opening of the door, stopped her walking up and down and stood looking at him, her cigarette in her hand.

He stopped, too, in the doorway, and stared at her. There was more wonder and astonishment in those fine blue eyes of his than I have ever before, I think, seen in any human eyes. It was altogether an extraordinary moment. He looked at Stella as Adam might have looked at the new-made Eve, long and incredulously and with complete amazement. Mankind, looking for the first time on womankind. There was awe in that look, and the deepest, most inexpressible gladness, and it moved me profoundly. I have said that Alan was a fine specimen of young manhood. The world tragedy had given his face a look of melancholy and resignation that had wonderfully refined it. It had hollowed his cheeks and eye-sockets; his forehead, his lips, seemed touched with the shadow of the world's doom. There was nothing in that face but what any woman with a heart must find lovable and endearing. He had always had a look of great fear lessness and courage, and stood as straight and tall as a young poplar. His hair was fair, much fairer than hers, and by comparison with his tall beauty she looked thick, sturdy, like a mountain pony. She had coloured, and she put her cigarette to her lips, once, a little nervously, then looked at me for an explanation. His appearance was so unexpected that I myself was startled and unprepared. I had made no plans in regard to him, though I meant, of course, to take him into our confidence sooner or later. I went to him and took his arm, and said:

"My dear Alan, I'd quite forgotten you might come back at any moment. In your absence, this miracle has happened. Don't ask questions now. Just look at her. She's flesh and blood. She's alive and well. Take her hand."

The two offered their hands to each other, ceremonially and in silence. Then Alan, knowing that something of importance had been interrupted by his entrance, said to me:

"Forgive me for breaking in on you. I heard a woman's voice. How could I help opening the door?" And he turned to leave the room. The Prime Minister stopped him.

"No, no, don't go," he said. I introduced Alan to him, saying that he was like a son to me and had been staying with me for some weeks. "That you're a friend of Dr. Selwyn's is proof enough of your discretion. We were trying to persuade" – he bowed towards Stella – "this lady to let us take her to the Palace and call out the late Queen's bodyguard to protect her. I myself think it the only proper and fitting place for her. She has been preserved by a miracle –"

"Do please be careful, Mr. Prime Minister, how you use that word," said Stella.

"– and we dare not risk exposing her, unprotected, to the public. Won't you add your persuasions to ours? Surely you see that it is the only thing to be done?"

"They want to make me into a sort of Queen," cried Stella, appealing to him. "It's ridiculous."

Alan did not make his reply directly to her, but to the Prime Minister. "It seems to me," he said, "that it's for her to decide. Her life is her own. We have no rights over her. Why try to persuade her against her will?"

"I want to stay here with Dr. Selwyn," said Stella.

"I'm sure Dr. Selwyn will be happy to have her under his care."

"Do you see any sense in my being a Queen?" she asked, once more appealing to him.

He answered her this time, meeting her eyes. "You're the most important person in the world," he said, "whether you wish to be or not. Does it matter what they call you?"

"But would you advise me to go?" she persisted.

"Advise you, yes. Persuade you, no, I wouldn't if I could. I think myself you'd be wise to go. It's the only way for you to be free. There's a garden there; there's even a lake. You could swim and run and walk and play games. Here you'd be a prisoner. There'd be no help for it."

"There's sense in that," she said. "Where have you come from? Have you just flown here from America?"

"I'm an American. I often come here. I flew here a few weeks ago."

She put out her cigarette thoughtfully, looked out of the window for a moment, and presently turned to us again with folded arms. I guessed that she had made up her mind to go.

"All right, I'll go and live at the Palace," she said, "but I shall do as I like when I'm there. I shall want plenty of books – "

"You will find the Palace library quite excellent, I think," said Mr. Hardy.

"– and I'd like a small observatory built for me in the grounds. I've always wanted to know something about the stars."

The Prime Minister took up his hat. "The Astronomer Royal will be at your disposal. May I suggest," he added, "that you come to the Palace tonight?"

"What about my nephew Freddie?" she asked. "Is he to stay here or may he come with me?"

"That's for you to decide, my dear," I said.

"Then I'll have him with me. He'll be company."

"I will expect the four of you at midnight," Mr. Hardy said.

"I will send my own car, and it will be followed, discreetly, by two or three secret service men in a second car. We must take no risks. I will be at the Palace, waiting for you. It will be best, I think, for you to come to the west entrance."

He begged us not to see him out, and shook hands, very warmly, with Alan. I guessed what was in his mind. He was already considering a position for him in the Government; something that would keep him near the Palace and in touch with Stella. I had never met him before that afternoon, but I did not find it difficult to understand his intentions.

Benglass was still out with the boy. Alan sat by the window, watching for his return, as we did not want him to surprise our secret until we were ready to tell him. Stella went into the kitchen to make tea for us. It was probably the last time, I thought, that she would perform this homely task, and I pitied her, for she was a simple person who would never take kindly to trappings and ceremony and much waiting on.

Much waiting on! It suddenly struck me for the first time – one's mind was constantly working along old, familiar lines, and constantly being pulled up short by the recollection that all things were changed – that she would have no women to wait on her. Were we to revert, then, to one of the customs of the harems? An unpleasant thought, but one that would have to be faced. Much else that was grievous and unpleasant would have to be faced. But of this more later.

We had tea on a balcony overlooking the street, where we could see without being seen. Alan's presence put a constraint upon Stella for she had no great love for men – and I could see her watching him when he was not looking at her. When she spoke of men, there was venom in the word. I don't know if she expected him to challenge these remarks, but he let them pass, without comment. Once when he went in to answer the telephone I asked her how much I might tell him of her story.

"Oh, everything, if you like," she said. "What does it matter? Tell him everything."

When Freddie returned and was told that he was to go to the Palace with his aunt, he behaved much as any other small boy would have behaved. He was enchanted with the idea, vociferously in love with it. Too young to be aware of doom or to keep tragedy long in mind, he now saw his life as a most diverting and surprising adventure. He took to Alan at once, as I guessed he would, and demanded that he also should go and live in the Palace. He looked very well in his new flannel suit and hat, and Stella was delighted with his appearance.

"It's worried me terribly," she said, "that he's had to go about looking such a ragamuffin, but what could I do?"

I now felt we might take Benglass into our confidence. He had been with me for many years, ever since my wife and I had returned from our long stay in China and Japan. He had been devoted to her, as he was later to Helen and Laura. When I told him the truth about the elder of my two guests he sank into a chair, and, like the Prime Minister, gave way to tears.

"To think," he sobbed, his face hidden in his hands, "that I should be privileged to look upon a woman again ... perhaps even to serve her in some way ... it's too much happiness!"

And, when he actually saw Stella, he also, like the Prime Minister, fell upon his knees.

"Oh, don't do that," she begged. "Do please get up. I don't want to be knelt to. It's absurd."

"Oh, madam!" he cried, and, reaching out his hand, he touched the hem of her trousers. This gesture made her smile in spite of herself, but she said, "If you don't get up I shall be angry."

I had never before seen my stolid old Benglass gave way to any emotion. He got to his feet clumsily, the tears pouring down his cheeks. "Forgive me, madam. I am overcome. Let me be your humble servant and slave. It's all I ask."

She held out her hand to him. "I hope we shall be good friends. I don't want any slaves. I'm just a very ordinary young woman, Benglass, and no one made any fuss about me until every other woman in the world died. So it isn't really a compliment you're paying me."

But such rational sentiments were beyond him, and he touched her hand as though it were the hand of a deity.

"Now, down we go," I said, looking at my watch. "The cars are here and it's time we were starting."

We drove rapidly through the bright streets, the police cars following close behind. Quite apart from the light of the powerful street-lamps there was always a soft glow from the many buildings, chiefly office buildings, which kept their lights on all night. They shone through the thick, semi-transparent glass and gave the city, after dark, a really lovely and fairy-like appearance.

The Palace, however, was not illuminated at all, and was merely a pale mass lying in the midst of the gardens that surrounded it.

It was a charming building, designed, like the Houses of Parliament, by Sir Wilfrid Lecomte, and at about the same time. It had a low, square, central tower supported by four still lower towers. To all these an effect of lightness and height had been given by the flat, fluted glass columns, in low relief, which ran from top to bottom between the windows. The whole building was softly coloured; it was the colouring of a pearl – a smoky pearl, perhaps – and to my mind it was by far the loveliest building in London.

The gate opened to us silently, and as silently closed again. As we drove through the courtyard, the lights of our cars showed us sentries standing on guard. We stopped at the west door, and there in the dim, candle-lit hall, Mr. Hardy and three members of the Cabinet were waiting for us, among them Mr. Devray, the Chancellor of the Exchequer and an old patient of mine. The other two, Mr. Ossuldon and Sir Bagot Wragg – known to his familiars as Ragbag – I knew only by name. Stella had to submit to a good deal of solemn hand-kissing, and a certain amount of emotion – the controlled, British variety – was displayed by all but Stella herself. She was growing, I could see, a little impatient, and wanted to see the Palace. Alan stood aloof and silent, and Freddie clung to his arm and took his cue from him.

The only servants we saw were two old men dressed in the Palace livery. At the moment, the Prime Minister said, there were only five altogether in the Palace, for he wished to get back as many of the late Queen's trusted staff as he could. He had already been fortunate enough, he told us, to find the chef, and he thought he would be able to get in touch with others later. He hoped that for the present these few would be sufficient to wait on Her Majesty and her young nephew.

"If you mean Freddie and me," said Stella, "don't you worry your head about us. We can take care of ourselves. And I do want to make this clear, once and for all. I'm not a Queen, and I'm not going to be a Queen, though I suppose I can't stop you if you insist on treating me like one. I'm Stella Morrow. I look upon this place as a sort of museum, and myself as a kind of museum-piece. I've come here because it's safe, and because I'm the only one of my kind, and because you say I've got to, and that's all."

"Quite candidly, my dear young lady," said Mr. Devray, who was always a blunt, outspoken man, "I don't see that you can help yourself. I fancy your choice will lie between being looked upon as a Queen and being looked upon as a goddess. Personally, I should much prefer the former. It's less aloof."

"I'll think it over," she said, smiling. "I hadn't considered being a goddess, and I rather like the sound of it. I've a good mind to be one."

I saw that she was quite ready to joke with Mr. Devray, and that she liked him better than Mr. Hardy, with his conventional, inflexible mind and frock-coated manners.

We all went up the great staircase, the two servants leading the way with the lighted candelabra. The rooms were already full of flowers, which, Mr. Hardy explained, he had had sent down from his country place in Buckinghamshire by air-car. (Have I remembered to say that this was the general mode of travel for short distances? These cars were slung from cables, and moved, by air power, at a tremendous rate and very comfortably. They travelled for the most part above the old railway-lines, now obsolete.)

Stella's large suite and Freddie's smaller one was connected by a library, an intimate and charming room lined with specially bound books.

"The choice of the late Queen," Mr. Hardy said, taking one of the candelabra himself and holding it above his head. "Any book you don't find here will doubtless be in the great library downstairs. I am sure that Mr. Riddlesdale, the late Queen's librarian, will be only too happy to take up his work here again."

A small table was laid for supper, and a champagne bottle was waiting, tilted in its nest of ice. Stella said she supposed it would be fitting for us all to drink one another's health, and more glasses were sent for. When the champagne was poured out, Mr. Hardy, showing a great deal of emotion and a surprising lack of tact, raised his and said, bowing to Stella:

"To you, ma'am, and to the future of England."

Stella raised hers and said, "To the end of this old world, amen, and the sooner the better."

"But, as long as the world lasts, to your very good health," said Mr. Devray.

"If my health needed any drinking to, I expect I wouldn't be here now," she answered, and emptied her glass.

"Will you suggest a toast, Mr. Holderness?" Mr. Hardy asked. "Mine doesn't seem to have met with much approval."

"Mine wouldn't either, I suspect," said Alan, "so I'll just propose a toast to our young friend, Master Fred Longstreet, who's really responsible, I gather, for our being here tonight."

Freddie grinned with pleasure and hardly knew which way to look. Then Mr. Ossuldon and Sir Bagot Wragg essayed appropriate little speeches, but, in spite of the efforts they made to preserve an appearance of calm, their emotions almost overcame them. Stella felt, and rightly, that it was time to put an end to so trying an occasion, and, the clock striking one just then, she said:

"Come, Freddie, you ought to have been asleep hours ago. Now that we know where our beds are, I think we'd better say good night and go to them."

"May you sleep well and comfortably," said Mr. Hardy. "You are safe here. And while I think of it, ma'am, don't be alarmed when you hear the church bells ringing and maroons and guns going off. The news is to be made public at nine o'clock tomorrow, but I myself, and doubtless Dr. Selwyn and Mr. Holderness, will be here before then. The public will naturally be very anxious to see you, so perhaps you'll step out on the balcony and say a few words to them from time to time. I imagine," he added, "that most of the population of England will try to catch a glimpse of you within the next few days. The police have already been informed, and will be prepared for immense crowds.

And if, tomorrow night, you'd consent to speak to the whole world on the air, you'd bring untold happiness to millions."

She looked at him with a sort of grudging admiration that was half sincere and half ironic.

"You've been enjoying yourself, Mr. Hardy," she said, "I can see that." And then she turned to me. "You'd better have left Freddie and me where we were, doctor, but I suppose there's no going back now. Well, good night, everybody."

We all left the Palace except Mr. Hardy, who, though he did not wish Stella to know, had moved his personal effects to a room in the West Tower and intended to sleep there permanently.

Alan and I walked home, as it was a fine night. I told him Stella's story as she had told it to me.

He said that for a woman like Stella, a woman who was above all things sincere, whole-hearted, and passionate, to receive such a blow as she had received was almost enough to unbalance her.

He had heard a good deal about Rainier, and thought he was now in New York. "A very brilliant fellow, I believe," he said, "but not to be trusted too far. However, he's planning some risky and spectacular experiment in his rocket car and hopes to die gloriously – or so I'm told."

He asked what had become of Hummel's papers, and I told him what I knew. He agreed with me that the matter of the stain must be gone into thoroughly, and at the earliest possible moment.

"So you, too, visualize a future for the world now?" I said.

"I'm going to fly to New York in a few days," he said, "to try and fetch Rainier back."

"My dear Alan, what for? She wouldn't look at him now, surely."

"She shall have the chance to, if she wants him. If she doesn't, she can tell him so. It may be crazy, but I want to talk to him, and I think she might have a word to say to him too. Anyhow, I'm going to do it, but I don't want her to know till it's done."

I tried to dissuade him, but his mind was made up, and, when Alan makes up his mind, one might as well save one's breath.

We were all at the Palace before nine the next morning. The world was like a sluggish ant-heap into which a stick was about to be poked. We went to the top of the Central Tower and watched the effect of the stick. At the first stroke of nine, all the bells in London began to ring, maroons were set off, and there was a continuous firing by the guns in the park. Everyone, we knew, would switch on his wireless at once, and those who were already in the streets would run to the public wireless-rooms to listen to the news.

People near the Palace had already guessed that something of importance was afoot, for police and mounted troops had earlier been posted along the routes that gave access to it, and up and down the Mall.

And presently, watching from the tower, we saw thousands of excited men hurrying towards the kiosks. Stella, at the thought of what was in store for her, began to look a little frightened.

"I don't want to say anything," she protested. "I couldn't possibly say anything to them. What can I say? 'Here I am?' They can see that for themselves."

She was wearing, this morning, a blue draped gown that reached half-way between knee and ankle. It was so long now since young women had worn stockings that I had almost forgotten the look of a pretty silk-clad leg. I hoped they would return to them again. The dress and the colour of it became her very well. It was her Sunday best, she said, seeing my eye on it, and she'd made it herself. We complimented her. I noticed that she barely looked at Alan, and still more rarely spoke to him, but there was no doubt that she was very conscious of his presence. I think she already guessed that the Prime Minister had his eye on him as a prospective husband for her, and she therefore took pains to show her complete indifference to him.

We switched on the wireless in the tower, and presently heard the announcer speak these words, in a voice well suited to the occasion:

"We are happy to proclaim glad tidings of world-wide importance. Let all the countries of the earth hear and know that in England today, well and safe and happy, and occupying her rightful place in the Palace as Queen of Great Britain, Queen of the League of English-Speaking Nations, Queen, indeed, if she wills it, of all nations, a woman sits enthroned, a woman blessed with youth and charm and intelligence, a veritable woman who, while she mourns her lost sisters, yet rejoices that she is able to bring, by the very fact of her existence, hope and joy once more to a dying and broken world.

"Her life was preserved by a miracle – by a miracle of science, perhaps, but a miracle nonetheless. The whole wonderful, thrilling story of her survival will be made public in due course. Meanwhile, men of all nations, give thanks to the God of All, Who, in His mercy, has conferred upon mankind this inestimable blessing. The flame of life is not dead. It still burns bravely, a tiny spark against the engulfing blackness of infinite night. Lift up your hearts and rejoice, for hope, hope is with us again!"

Stella turned to Mr. Hardy.

"Congratulations," she said ironically. "It's all yours, every word of it. I'm beginning to recognize your touch."

No sooner was the announcement made than the air was filled with shouts and cries and rejoicings. Men yelled the news to one another. "There's a woman alive!" "There's a woman alive in the Palace!" "There's a woman in the Palace!" "A woman in the Palace." "A woman, alive!" The hubbub grew and grew as the great rush for the Palace began. Men came running from every direction at first, but in such numbers that they soon formed a mass that thickened and then congealed and moved scarcely at all, but was added to at the edges until it became solid and reached really terrifying proportions. London, the suburbs, the towns and villages, were all drained to make up that living flood. Hastily improvised signs and the amplified voices of traffic control men urged them to keep moving slowly past the front of the

Palace, but the movement was so slow as to be barely perceptible. All that day and the next Stella hardly left the balcony, and even snatched hurried meals there, for if she went away for more than a few minutes there was a clamour from those who had at last pushed their way to the great gates and had not yet seen her. Now and again she would cry out, "Yes, it's all true! Here I am, and thank you for being pleased about it!" The cheering was incessant. The first night the crowd merely thinned a little, but did not disperse. Stella didn't undress, but lay down and slept from time to time, coming out on the flood-lit balcony at intervals to smile and wave. The second day was even worse than the first. Thousands of hats were continually flung in the air, a sea of arms waved, men shouted and yelled themselves hoarse. Many fainted, and had to be passed over the heads of the crowd, and a rough passage they must have had to the ambulances, far on the outskirts of the throng. I kept a watchful eye on Stella to see that she wasn't overdoing it, but she stood the strain extremely well.

At about five o'clock on the afternoon of the second day, a plane flew overhead and let fall showers of paper. We thought this was some new device of Mr. Hardy's at first, but he denied it, and, seeing that the papers were printed leaflets, he hurriedly sent out for some. Even before they could be brought to us, a change had come over the crowd. The cheering ceased, and a loud and ominous murmuring and muttering took its place. The leaflets, thousands of which were now in the hands of the crowd, had been hastily printed, and read like this:

"Men! You are easily fooled. This is not a woman at all, but a boy dressed up. It is a shameful trick on the part of the British Prime Ministre for the glory of Britain. There are no women. Go back to your homes. It is nothing but a hoax, perfidious and indecent."

"One of our friends across the Channel," said Mr. Hardy, indicating the spelling of "Minister" and the word "perfidious." "What sceptics they always were! And never more so than when we had nothing to hide! But I'm afraid it will be a trifle difficult to disprove the charge. There is little we can do now but to disperse the crowd before it grows ugly and unmanageable, as it very soon will."

One of our own planes had already driven off the disbelieving intruder, who returned the way he had come, leaving a broad trail of scattered leaflets behind him. In a few moments Mr. Hardy's fears began to prove well founded. Bits of gravel and small missiles were thrown at the guard, and someone hurled an orange at a policeman, knocking his helmet off. Scuffles began, and turned into fights. "Rush the gates!" a man yelled, and at once the cry was taken up. The crowds surged against the ironwork, and Mr. Hardy sent Stella in. Angry shouts and menaces grew louder moment by moment. Word was hastily sent to the Air Ministry, and soon light planes carrying those harmless and highly efficacious "happy gas bombs" began to circle low about the Palace. These so-called "bombs," which did no more harm when they fell than paper bags filled with flour might have done, were dropped with great accuracy into the thickest of the crowd, and, exploding at a touch, released a gas which was the invention of a clever and good-natured American. It rendered the most excited trouble-makers happy and tractable. A jovial, careless good-temper took the place of anger. Men began to laugh at nothing at all and at everything, and regarded themselves and each other as highly and irresistibly humorous. So agreeable were the effects of the gas that few thought of wearing a mask to protect themselves from it. Besides, there was something instantly laughter-provoking in the mere act of donning a mask in order to preserve one's bad temper, and the sight of anyone so doing usually sent the rest of the crowd into fits of delighted mirth. (Sir Bagot Wragg had once released one of these bombs at a Cabinet meeting, with the happiest results.)

So the great gathering began to disperse, amiably enough. It took from one to two hours for the effect of the gas to wear off, and by the time it did there was usually an actual change of feeling. Now there were shouts of, "Whoopee! She may be a King or a Queen, but she's a good lad," and "We had a fine trip from Blackpool, anyhow," and "Congratulations, Mr. Hardy. How are you today, and is it a boy or a girl?" and "All right for you chaps; just you wait till next April Fools' Day, that's all." There were many equally genial but less repeatable remarks. Gradually the great spaces about the Palace cleared, and I don't mind admitting that we all breathed sighs of relief. The planes were ordered to stand by, in case of further trouble, and at eight o'clock another wireless proclamation was made.

"Some of our friends across the Channel have cast doubts upon the existence of a woman in the Palace. These may have been genuine doubts, or they may have been inspired by jealousy. You have indeed been the victims of a hoax, but only by the visitor who dropped the leaflets. Countless thousands of you saw Stella Morrow – Queen Stella to us – with your own eyes, and heard her voice. Your unbelief might well seem an insult to a very gracious lady, but she understands and forgives. She herself will speak to you on the air at nine o'clock this evening."

By this time an evening paper was being circulated, bearing on its front page an enormous coloured photograph of Stella – she had sat for it at noon – and a short account of the genius, Hummel, whose skill had preserved her life, and who had so tragically lost his own. There were still doubters, but the majority believed because they wished to believe.

At nine, Stella, wearing a new gown speedily made for her by Stenka, the late Queen's dress maker, was seen and heard by millions.

"It's quite true," she said, speaking without a sign of nervousness, "I'm alive and well, thanks to a wonderful doctor. Someday we'll all be using the stain – you can read about it in the papers – and then perhaps we'll never be ill anymore. You'll want to know what it feels like, I expect, to be the only woman in the world. Well, it's perfectly horrible. I used to be games mistress at Miss Blount's school. How we all wish we could turn back the clock! A world without women is no world at all, but we must live out our lives somehow, and try to make the best of things. I'm going to study the stars. I advise you all to study something. It will take your minds off our present troubles. The thing to do, I am sure, is to keep occupied. Good night."

She soon gained confidence on the air, and began to speak her mind. Two nights later she gave a talk which startled Mr. Hardy.

"We women," she said, "haven't done nearly as much as we ought to have done. It isn't that we're not strong enough. Women are strong. They're often tougher than men, and can stand more. In some countries they used to do all the hard work. Women could always do what men wanted them to do, and be what men wanted them to be. That was the trouble with us. We always wanted to please men. That was our undoing. If men went to war, we played up to them. The music and the marching and the uniforms helped, of course. That was what they were for. If men had gone off to fight in their everyday clothes, we'd have seen the silly business for what it was, and we'd have had something to say about it! Late in the nineteenth century we made a lot of fuss and changed things just a bit, but when we'd got a good deal of what we wanted, what did we do with it? Nothing very wonderful. Why? Because we knew men didn't really want us to. H.G. Wells used to write novels about women who were super-women. They were grand women, but you could never make yourself believe that the men really liked them. Wells didn't really believe it either. Well, you may ask, would that matter? It would matter terribly to men. You see, you men insist on feeling romantically about us. You are hopeless romantics.

"Let me tell you in strict confidence, we've got a romantic Prime Minister. Now, I think that is very dangerous, because romantic people are nearly always bloody-minded. That's the reverse side of the picture. If you're romantic, you like the idea of war and killing. Why, heaven knows. Perhaps I will know if I think about it long enough. But it's true that romance and killing have always gone hand in hand. I'm not romantic. I think life is sacred. All life – yours, mine. I'm a realist. I believe in love – the universal kindness.

"The reason that all this came into my mind is that I saw a dead man this morning. He tried to get into the Palace. I think myself it was just curiosity, but the guards thought he had designs on my life and shot him. I heard the noise and ran out. Well, there he lay, dead, with all his secrets and his hopes and thoughts destroyed. A wonderful, complicated creature that to save our souls we couldn't make, or even give life to again. A silly gun went 'Bang!' and there he was. His life or mine, Mr. Hardy said. Well, I don't know. He wasn't armed. Why couldn't I have talked to him? If things like this are going to happen because of me, I'd better not be here."

Mr. Hardy reproached her for her criticisms of him, but she told him that if he insisted on regarding her as Queen of Great Britain and of the world, she must be permitted to say what she pleased.

So interested was Alan in the developments at the Palace that he postponed his trip to America from day to day, and I began to hope that he would change his mind and not go at all.

Stella settled down to a sort of routine, which was only broken by the arrival of important persons from home or abroad who begged to be allowed to see her. It presently became the custom to invite such visitors either to lunch or dinner, and hardly a day now passed without from fourteen to twenty sitting down to table. Lunch was always an informal meal – Mr. Hardy had some difficulty in persuading Stella to observe any formalities whatever – and to it came musicians, dramatists, scientists, artists, actors, diplomats, businessmen. Thanks to the universally adopted Basic English, language was no bar to conversation, and Stella liked nothing better than to get them all talking. She had no shyness, would speak her mind freely, and didn't in the least mind being put in the wrong. She knew little about art and less about music, but was amused and instructed by the conflicting opinions of those who thought they did. Only the painters and the scientists, it appeared, were going on with their work as before. The happiest, most absorbing, and pleasantest of all the arts furnishes its own rewards. The world might end, but painters went on painting because it was so much pleasanter to paint than not to paint. Scientists, too, were able to forget mankind's doom in their researches, their almost divine interest and passion for truth providing momentum enough to carry them through even such a monstrous tragedy as this. Writers require readers, especially women readers, and like to picture a posterity for their books; poets live chiefly in a future, in a *becoming* world, and their voices were now silenced. As for businessmen, they had little enough to live for, with no new prospectuses coming out, and perhaps a directors' meeting once a month and an hour or two at the office each day if their businesses were fortunate enough to survive at all. The rest of their time was spent at golf or bridge, unless they had other hobbies. (Gardeners, like painters and scientists, continued to function with a scarcely diminished enthusiasm, and there were horticultural shows all through that summer.) As for racing and prize-fighting, they went on almost as before; in fact, the various rings were crowded every night.

Stella and Freddie swam in the lake each morning. (Alan sometimes joined them, to please the boy, breakfasting in the flat on his return.) They then did setting-up exercises, and by ten o'clock Stella was ready to meet Mr. Hardy and the Cabinet. They now made a point of consulting her about everything, though rarely, at first, listening to her advice. She soon changed all that.

Stella had invited Alan to go to the Palace whenever he pleased. "No ceremony," she said. "Come when you like." She treated him, when there, with a sort of brisk friendliness – "her games-mistress manner," Alan called it – but took pains to show no special interest in him, and rarely allowed herself to be alone with him for more than a minute or two. When Mr. Hardy was there, her manner became still more off-hand. I think Alan understood her far too well to be offended by this. He not only understood her, he admired her unreservedly, and I could see that she interested him deeply. In fact, so absorbed was he in what was going on at the Palace, so fascinated by the spectacle of Stella overriding Mr. Hardy's prejudices and keeping the Cabinet in its place, that I think he sometimes regretted his decision. He was in almost constant touch with New York by telephone, and was having inquiries made into Rainier's whereabouts.

"As soon as I can get on his track," he said, "I'm off."

One morning he was rung up from San Francisco, and as the result of his talk he went to the landing-ground and spent the morning tuning up his machine. Rainier, he told me, had been traced to the Pacific coast, where he was believed to be living under another name.

"I don't know what he's up to," he said, "but I'll find him now. I'll say goodbye to Stella this afternoon, and start first thing tomorrow morning. If he's alive by the time I get there, I'll bring him back. By the way," he added, "I wish you'd persuade Stella while I'm gone that Freddie ought to be at school. She's got an absurd prejudice against schools, but he'll be much happier there than being tutored by Riddlesdale in the Palace. Only don't say I put you up to it."

When he told her he was going to America for a while and bade her goodbye, she refrained from asking him why he was going or when he was coming back. She pretended not to be missing him, too, but I was not deceived by this. This boy Freddie made no such pretences, and was disconsolate.

There was one subject on which she would allow no one to speak to her – except, very occasionally, myself – and that was marriage. And it was, of course, the subject that was uppermost in everyone's mind. No, she vowed to me, in private, she would never marry, never bring children into such a world.

The human race had made one blunder too many; let it take its punishment and end. All sorts of people tried to approach her, hoping to convince her of the terrible mistake she was making, but as soon as she learnt what they had come for she changed the subject, or dismissed them. The Archbishop of Canterbury tried again and again, and Mr. Hardy had brought up the subject so often that he was now forbidden to speak of it.

"You brought it on yourselves," she repeated, "with your strutting and your bragging and your drum-beating and your vaingloriousness. And now you dare to come to me and say, 'Let's begin all over again.' No, no, really, you're asking too much. I refuse to listen to another word."

In some countries men were trying to outdo the vice and libertinism of Rome in its worst days, and making a parade of it. In England and America and the League of English-Speaking Nations generally, such behaviour was severely punished, as indeed it was discouraged and frowned upon in most of the European countries. It was an offence here for men to masquerade as women, as numbers were quite ready to do, their excuse being that the eye wearied of but one sort of dress, and that men craved the illusion, at least, that there were still women in the world. Mr. Hardy would have none of it, and in those countries where it was permitted or ignored, order and discipline of any sort were soon overthrown.

He fostered all outdoor sports and contests and tried to revive the glories of the Olympic Games. He offered money prizes for records of all sorts, and urged men not to despair of reaching the moon and Mars, and returning from them in safety. Many had made the attempt in the past, but had never been heard of again. Whether they fell eventually into the sea, or reached their objectives and died there, or went hurtling for ever through outer space, no one knew.

Then one day, after an absence of more than a month, Alan returned. He appeared at my flat without sending me word of his coming, and he was alone. He told me he had spent some fruitless weeks searching for Rainier in San Francisco, and had at last traced him to Honolulu, where he was making some adjustments, in secret, to his new rocket car. He was determined, it appeared, to be the first man to reach the moon and return again, and dreaded that someone might succeed before he did.

Alan reached Honolulu just too late to speak to him. He arrived at the very moment that Rainier and a young scientist named Bodenthorp, who had decided to accompany him, were taking off. At one moment the huge, torpedo-like monster was in sight, resting on a concrete base, its nose pointing upward. Then there was a roar that deafened the ears and shook the ground and the place where it had been was empty. Alan got into his plane again and flew back to England.

"If I'd been fifteen minutes sooner," he said, "I believe I could have brought him back with me. My own fault for not having gone at once."

"But what good would it have done?" I asked him.

"It would have been chiefly for my own satisfaction," he said.

He went to the Palace with me later in the day, and saw Stella. I told him he'd better see her alone, and, catching sight of Mr. Hardy in the grounds, I joined him and went for a stroll. About half an hour later I thought they would have finished their talk and I went up to the library.

As soon as I opened the door I realized that they had been having an argument, and that Stella was angry and indignant. Seeing me, she called out, "Come in, doctor. You'd better stay and hear what he's got to say for himself." But I went to the far end of the room and took up a book, saying, "Finish your talk. I'll sit here by the window till it's over."

I couldn't help hearing what they were saying even then, though I tried not to. She was very angry with him – as I had fully expected – for having attempted to find Rainier and bring him back.

"What has he to do with me now," she demanded, "or I with him? If he had wanted to see me he would have come here himself. but he didn't want to, any more than I wanted to see him. Why didn't you ask my permission first? Surely it's my own affair? All this plotting and planning behind my back – I dislike it. I hate it."

"It seemed to me," Alan said, "very important that you should see him, as he's the cause of your determination not to marry. And that," he added, "concerns everyone, myself included."

"And what good would it have done if I had seen him?"

"It might have helped you to realize the folly of judging all men by one. Or, on the other hand, you might have found your feelings towards him had not changed, in which case you might have married him."

"Now that I am the only woman in the world," she said bitterly, "you think he might have had a change of heart. Thank you."

"I think you're being petty," he said, "and there is too much at stake for pettiness. Your refusal to consider marriage is based on frivolous and personal grounds, and it's quite unworthy of you."

"What business is this of yours?" she demanded, with an indignation that seemed to me a little forced and unreal.

"What business is it of mine?" he repeated. Then he answered her, very quietly, with a quotation from Cicero: "'I care more for that long age I shall not see than for the little that I hold of time.'"

She was silent for a moment, then she said, "Very pretty! Very apropos! Very impersonal and noble! So you think I ought to marry, do you? You think I ought to go on with this business?"

"I do," he said.

"Why should I? What if I honestly think it had better end?"

He was silent, and I guessed that he was looking at her with that straight and candid look I knew so well.

"Would you marry, if you were me?" she demanded.

"I can't answer that. If I were you, I suppose I'd be asking the very question you're asking me. I presume I should get the same answer."

"Oh, you don't help me. You know what I feel. I've told you again and again. I've no love for men. It's not what one of them did to me, in spite of what you think. It's what they've done to the world; the mess they've made of things; their awful folly and stupidity and cruelty."

"You've got to share the blame. You followed us like a lot of sheep. And there have always been mothers as well as fathers."

"That's true." There was a long silence; then she said, very rapidly, as though she feared she would recall the words even as she spoke them, "Well, why don't you take on the job yourself?"

"What job?" he asked her.

She answered, still with that breathless haste: "Whatever you like to call it – partner, husband."

My heart nearly stopped beating. For a long fraction of a second I dreaded that Alan might make some answer that would chill, anger, or hurt her. But he responded to that bravely flung out suggestion quickly and frankly.

"I'm yours if you want me. Gladly. If I have any doubts, it's because someone else might..."

"Might what?" she asked sharply.

"Might make you happier. Might make you a better husband."

"You think that matters?"

"Most certainly."

"Just as though we were an ordinary couple in an ordinary world?"

"Precisely the same. Why not?"

Then she remembered – I'm sure she had forgotten – that I was in the room. She turned towards me. "Doctor," she called out, in a voice unlike her own, "did you hear? Did you hear?"

I took off my glasses.

"Yes, my dear," I said.

"What do you think of it, then?"

"Need you ask that?"

Suddenly she sat down in a chair by the writing-table, dropped her head on her arms, and burst into tears. I went to her and stroked her hair.

"I'm all right," she said at last. "Only – those poor children of ours – and their poor children – think of the awful loneliness! Have we any right...? Isn't it cruel of us...?"

Alan was standing beside her, not touching her, yet within touch. "I don't know," he said. "I've always thought the Swiss Family Robinson had a grand time. I always envied them."

She gave a little laugh and began to wipe her eyes.

"Well, don't let's tell Mr. Hardy," she said, still tearful, "until Alan and I have had a chance to get used to each other. He'll only gloat, and so pompously. I dread it. And, Alan, listen to me."

She faced him, tears still wet on her cheeks. "And I want you to be a witness, doctor, because this is important. I don't love you, Alan, and I don't expect love from you. I respect you. I think you're a fine sort of person, and I admire your appearance and your health. I don't want ugly children, and, if I married someone as ugly as I am myself, they might be ugly. If we come to love each other someday, so much the better, but I shall look on it as a kind of miracle, and I shall neither ask it nor expect it, you may be sure of that. It's best to be quite frank, I think. If I've got to marry, and you all seem to think I must, I'd rather marry you than anybody, and I'm very grateful to you for being willing."

She pushed back her chair and got up. "Now I've said my say."

"Now I'll say mine," he answered. "I respect and admire you more than I can say. I don't know whether I love you or not. And what does it matter? If I did, I'd certainly be loving you quite differently in a year's time, and you'll seem quite a different person to me. If you're making a sacrifice – and I know you are – so am I. My position isn't going to be a very easy one, and it has its ridiculous side as well. But never mind about that: we must have something to laugh at."

He held out his hand to her, smiling, and she put her hand into it. Then we heard voices in the hall outside, and they moved apart. A moment later, Mr. Hardy was announced, and he came in looking more than ordinarily serious. He was a slender man with stooping shoulders, thin and colourless hair, and a deeply lined face. It was a somewhat Roman face, and busts of Mr. Hardy, especially in bronze, looked amazingly like him.

He kissed Stella's hand, and said without preamble:

"A very grave situation has arisen, ma'am. I am calling a meeting of the Cabinet at once to discuss it. They'll be here in half an hour or so, and meanwhile, with your permission, I will put the facts before you as briefly as possible."

"Do," she said, "and as quickly."

We all sat down, and he explained what had happened rapidly and clearly. The situation, it appeared, was this. A certain nation which I shall not name here, very strong and great, and outside both the United States of Europe and the League of English-Speaking Nations, had put forward a candidate for Stella's hand.

They claimed that it was for the good of the future that their blood should be mingled with the blood of posterity. So strongly did they feel about the matter that if their proposal were ignored or declined they threatened to look upon it as an insult and an act of hostility, and declare war. They had over fifty thousand planes ready to take the air, and every man in them was ready to die for the future of his race.

"Assuming that you would wish me to do so," said the Prime Minister, "I have drafted a reply which amounts to a categorical refusal. I have at the same time informed their ambassador that our strength in the air is no less than theirs, and that if they resort to force we shall know how to protect ourselves and you."

"Is that really the way you intend to deal with the situation?" Stella asked.

"How else?" he replied. "The tone they have adopted is one that leaves no other course open to us."

"I should imagine that there were several courses open to us. Where's the ambassador?"

"In Downing Street, waiting for a reply. Of course, you realize that this is virtually an ultimatum, and that when we refuse, as we must refuse, he will hand in his papers and fly back to his own country at once. Then hostilities will begin. On the other hand, it will probably mean a victory for our forces, for we can undoubtedly count on the active support of the rest of the League."

"But I want to see him," said Stella. "I want to talk to him. I know him quite well. He's been here twice to lunch, and once to dinner. Is this the first intimation they've given that they want to produce a husband for me? It seems very sudden."

Mr. Hardy admitted that approaches had been made, not only by the country in question, but by a number of the other countries as well.

"And why haven't I been told?"

"You will remember, ma'am, that you have expressly forbidden me to speak to you on the subject of marriage. I have disobeyed you today only because of the threat of war."

"Now that's trifling, Mr. Hardy, really it is," she said indignantly. "You know perfectly well that I want to be kept informed of what's going on, and it's most important that I should have been told of these offers. It was simply that I got sick and tired of being pestered by you and the Archbishop and all the members of the Cabinet. Dr. Selwyn's been nearly as bad. I had to put a stop to it. But this is quite different, and I ought to have known of it. Imagine letting things go so far! I could have prevented it quite easily."

"I'm sorry you accuse me of trifling, ma'am. You are as difficult to deal with as Queen Elizabeth herself." Mr. Hardy began to put his papers away, and, seeing that he was hurt, Stella said:

"Now, Mr. Hardy, you know I'm quite fond of you and I realize your difficulties perfectly well. But I still think it was silly. When can I see the ambassador?"

Mr. Hardy said he could be there in five minutes, but he was strongly opposed to her meeting him. He had become very overbearing, he said, and might even be rude.

"I don't mind if he is. I can deal with rudeness. Some of the girls at the school, when they first came, used to try being rude. Besides, why should he be? He doesn't know yet what I'm going to say." Mr. Hardy eventually gave in, though with reluctance, and the ambassador was sent for. Alan and I thought we had better go, but she insisted that we stay. "I'd like you to hear what he says," she told us.

We had not long to wait.

He was a thick, fat, swarthy little man with an oily skin and a large head, which he carried thrust forward rather in the manner of a tortoise. His small eyes were very quick, however, and very shrewd.

Unattractive he certainly was, but he managed to be impressive. Stella went to meet him, smiling and holding out her hand. He kissed it, and, at her request, sat down.

"Well," Stella said, "this is all very unexpected and surprising. You see, I'd forbidden poor Mr. Hardy to speak to me of marriage because I was so sick of the whole subject. You can imagine how they've all been at me about it. So he simply hasn't dared to mention the matter to me since, and consequently I hadn't heard of your previous offers. I'm very flattered indeed, but the truth is I don't want to get married at all, and, if I ever do marry, I'd rather like to please myself."

The ambassador bowed and made regretful gestures.

"As to wanting or not wanting, madam," he said, "surely one does not consult one's personal feelings in such a matter. No, no. Surely one does not. *It is necessary that you marry*. There is nothing more to be said."

"But is it necessary?" Stella asked. "I don't agree that it is. After all, except for an extraordinary combination of circumstances, I wouldn't be here at all."

"That, madam, is equally true of any of us," said the ambassador, with perfect justice.

She laughed.

"You've scored a point there, but you know what I mean. By rights I ought to be dead. Why not just forget all about me? To all intents and purposes, the world has ended. Well, I say, let it end, and good riddance. Unfortunately, I find that very few of you agree with me."

"The world must not end," said the ambassador, very slowly.

"It's all very well your saying it mustn't end," replied Stella with spirit, "but if it hadn't been for the skill of a little quack doctor it *would* have ended. That you can't deny. Besides, why should *you* care? You're talking about ending it for millions of men by making war. How can you be so illogical?"

"All the men of my country," said the ambassador, giving emphasis to each word, "will gladly give up their lives to provide for a future in which our race shall play its proper part."

"Then the more fools they. And what is this proper part?"

He answered:

"It is a great pity you are not of my nation. Even though you are not, you will marry one of the men of my nation. The future will then be ours. It is fitting and right that it should be so."

"I'm sorry to find," she said, "that you're still primitive enough and unenlightened enough to believe in killing as a solution to any problem. Our schoolchildren know better than that. Killing solves nothing, Mr. Ambassador. Nothing. And before I will allow men to fight over me, I will gladly put an end to my own life. That I'm quite determined on. And then where's your future?"

He once more bowed and made the same regretful gestures.

"We must do what we can. We may fail. Still, we must try."

Stella looked at him in amazement.

"It boils down to this," she said. "You'd rather the world had no future at all than that yours shouldn't be the predominant race in it?"

"That is so."

"But suppose every other nation were to feel the same way?"

He moved his heavy shoulders, his short neck seemed to sink between them.

"Then the strongest will succeed."

"And you believe yourself to be the strongest?"

"It might seem boastful, madam, if I were to say so."

"But, then, supposing that when all the fighting is over, and thousands and thousands had been slaughtered, you found me dead – as I promise you I would be – what then?"

He chose to evade this question. "If I were in your happy position, madam, may I tell you what I would do?"

"By all means."

"I would go away to a safe place and I would say to the nations of the world, 'Fight for me. The strongest shall have me.' And I would choose a man of the victorious nation, and marry him. Then it would indeed be a case of the survival of the fittest, and justice would attend the birth of the new world."

"But how wasteful!" Stella said. "Why not choose one man from each nation and set them to fighting for me?"

"That would not be sufficiently final and conclusive."

"Well, Mr. Ambassador," she said, "I know of a far better and fairer way. You see, I am not at all convinced that manliness or virility or fitness to survive can be demonstrated by the number, violence, or deadliness of the bombs that can be dropped on the helpless populations of towns and villages. I confess that I simply cannot see the connection. No, no. I have a better idea, if you will forgive my saying so. If I marry – please note that I still say 'if,' though if I saw any hope of peace between the nations I'd be much more inclined to it – if I marry I shall hope to be blessed with a large family of daughters. Now I intend to see to it that each one of my daughters marries a member of a different race or nation, but they shall only marry men of those nations I think worthy of preservation. Worthy, that is, because of their value to the world and to civilization, or because of some peculiar racial genius. In some home in your own land, Mr. Ambassador, there is a motherless boy who may one day be the husband of one of my daughters. The choice shall be left to you; I only ask that he may be brought up here in the Palace, under my own care and supervision, from the age of six years. You shall, of course, see him at regular intervals, or appoint someone you trust to see him. I will give the greatest possible care and thought to his upbringing, in order to fit him for the role he will some day be called upon to play."

The ambassador considered the matter, appeared to be satisfied, and complimented her on her diplomacy. When she stood up, to show that the interview was at an end, he kissed her hand and said, "I will give your message to my people. They will be gratified. When the time comes, madam, be sure you will be reminded of your promise."

And the swarthy, thick little man bowed himself out.

"Well," Stella, turned to us, "that was all right, wasn't it?"

"Excellent," said Mr. Hardy. "I hope you realize, however, that such a promise could have been made by no one but yourself. Some such solution came into my mind at once, but I could hardly barter your possible daughters for the price of peace. And while we are on the subject, ma'am, may I ask if you propose to keep your promise to him?"

"I hope I shall always keep my promises," she answered. "But I think I said, 'There is a motherless boy who may one day be the husband,' and so on."

"You did," Alan and I told her.

"He will want it in writing," said Mr. Hardy. "You may be sure of that."

"Don't let's meet trouble half-way, Mr. Hardy," she protested. "At least I've made a bridge. You seem ready to leap in the rapids."

"I think a woman's motto has always been," said Mr. Hardy, "'A problem deferred is a problem solved.'"

"And a man's, 'Fighting is better than thinking,'" she retorted.

"I think there's a Chinese motto," remarked Alan, "which says, 'He who generalizes about women shall find his head in a bag.'"

That night Stella spoke on the wireless as usual, and frankly.

"Some nations, I hear," she said, "are taking up a war-like attitude. I must marry one of their citizens, they say, or they will fight. Others talk of fighting to gain possession of me. Really, really! It is enough to drive one to despair. I warn you, as I have warned you before, that I will put an end to my own life rather than be the cause of bloodshed. And when you talk so grandly about fighting, what do you mean, you men? You mean sending out planes to drop bombs on the people of another country. Do you call that fighting? It's like a small boy spitting out of a window on the heads of passers-by, and just about as glorious. Shame on you! Really, I despair of you. I have the greatest respect and admiration for your intelligence. You are the thinkers, the inventors, the innovators, the explorers, not we. But you are also confirmed and incurable mischief-makers, and as by your mischief-making you undo all the good by your inventing and exploring and thinking, you've got to be kept under. If I marry and have children, and their children begin a new world, there will only be one man to every three or four women. I'm convinced that it's the only way. The logic men show as individuals they entirely lose in groups. With women it may be the other way round, which will be far less dangerous. Now let me hear no more of this war talk or I won't marry at all. Good night."

For the next few weeks she and Alan played tennis, swam, talked, walked about the grounds, and spent every available moment in each other's society. Mr. Hardy was fairly rubbing his hands with delight as he watched them from his window. Stella was still unaware that he was living in the Palace, and, as it was for her own safety and protection, I had agreed not to tell her. I hoped he would have sufficient tact to pretend surprise when she told him her news.

Daily, vast crowds surged about the Palace gates. They came from all countries, they made pilgrimages from the four quarters of the earth, and at appointed times Stella would step out on the balcony, show herself, and say a few words. Men the world over now believed in and accepted her. She became, as Mr. Devray had predicted, more than a woman to them, more than a Queen. She became a Goddess. One day Mr. Hardy was told by the Archbishop of Canterbury that certain religious groups not only abroad but even in England were claiming for her a supernatural origin. When Mr. Hardy warned her of this she considered how she might put a stop to it, and that same night gave a talk on the air about her early life.

"My father and mother," she said, "were, as I have told you before, farming people. They were married at the little parish church of Wonnup, near Stroud, in Gloucestershire. At the wedding a funny thing happened. An old man stood up just as the service was about to begin and said that the marriage must not take place, as my father was already married and had a wife in Newcastle. It appeared that the old man was very deaf, and, having mistaken the date, thought that he was at the wedding of another couple who were to be married the following day. His error was pointed out to him, and so great was his embarrassment and chagrin that he then and there made my parents the present of a very fine Alderney cow. The cow was named Stella, and when I appeared upon the scene they named me, their first-born, after her."

Stella's face, which I have described to you, now became the pattern for all female beauty. She sat – unwillingly enough – for sculptors, painters, and photographers. Her proportions and measurements became those of the ideal woman. She accepted it all with amused tolerance, and once said, with a laugh, "This world is full of surprises, but that I should have ousted the Venus de Milo is the most surprising of all."

A new star was discovered at Mount Wilson and named Stella Morrow. Soon the five-pointed star became everywhere the popular sign and symbol. A new flag was made and flown in all countries, and the device was a bright red star rising out of a blue sea against a background of white. Prayers for Stella's health and safety were said daily in the churches, and gradually a sort of Stella-worship grew up in primitive countries and among the less educated. When she heard that in some lands statues of her had been placed in temples and were being sacrificed to, she was angry and disgusted, and said that such doings were to be discouraged by every possible means.

"It will go on in secret, I'm afraid," said Mr. Hardy.

"Oh, well," she said, on considering the matter, "all that nonsense will die out when the doers themselves die. I suppose it isn't worth worrying about, really. And perhaps it's a sort of outlet for the poor souls. The great thing about the new world will be this: that every nation will have the same start. There'll be no backward countries. There'll be a divergence of speech and custom, I suppose, in time, but as the world will all be linked up by air and wireless, I doubt if it will go very far. It will be a pleasantly homogeneous world."

"I only regret that I shan't be here to see it," said Mr. Hardy.

"He doesn't mean a word of it," Stella said, turning to me. "In a world where women are in the majority, he'd have a wretched life, and he knows it."

"I've never been much in favour of polygamy myself," said Mr. Devray, who was also present. "I don't think men are as a rule. They know they'd feel too spied upon."

The day Stella announced over the wireless that she was going to marry, the whole world went mad with joy. It seemed to have been waiting for this withheld breath, and the word released a vast amount of pent-up emotion, and came as a relief and a message of hope to millions. There was a universal pealing of bells and a booming of guns and a screaming of sirens; young men built bonfires on hills the world over, and young and old celebrated the great news with torchlight processions, revels, and public festivals. Mr. Hardy, whom she informed of her decision only a few hours before she made it public, played his part well enough, and even shed genuine tears of thankfulness. He had had his eye on Alan since the first day they met. He admired, trusted, and liked him whole-heartedly, as a man who is devious and something of an opportunist likes and admires – with a touch of envy – one whose candour and straightforwardness are natural to him and beyond question.

The date was fixed for July 15th, and soon the whole country, and later the entire civilized world, was clamouring for a royal wedding. The young couple, men insisted, should be crowned King and Queen as part of the marriage ceremony. In fact, a simultaneous marrying and crowning seemed to be the wish of all. But Stella and Alan firmly refused to be crowned, and at her next talk on the air Stella gave her reasons.

"It complicates things too much," she said, "and it would all have to be dropped later on. You can't have a lot of Princes and Princesses chopping wood and cleaning pots and pans, and doing their own cooking. I understand quite well why you want it, but if you stop to think about it you'll realize that it's out of the question. In a highly organized and complex world, Kings and Queens have their uses. They're ornamental, and they keep things tidy and civilized, and in this country they've played a most valuable part. But in such a world as I foresee, there would be no place for them – or not for hundreds and hundreds of years. Work out for yourselves, if you haven't already done so, what the population will probably be one hundred years from now. If Alan and I have the good fortune to have eight daughters – and we might even aspire to ten or twelve – and each of them marries and has, let us say, an average of six children per couple, and *their* children marry – yes, the second generation will have to marry first cousins, but there's no harm in that if they're healthy – you can estimate for yourselves the number of people there will be living on the earth in one or two hundred years' time. It will be a busy, self-contained little colony, with lots to do and to learn, and lots to teach to their children. And pretty soon little colonies will break off from it and go flying off to make other colonies. And so the world will gradually become repopulated again. It will be a slow business, but, after all, there's no great hurry. You'll wonder how these men and women of the future will know how to build planes and make machines and re-conquer the earth for human beings again. Well, our most valuable knowledge is to be stored and preserved and made accessible to future generations. And how best to do this is now going to be our chief problem: what to keep and how to keep it. We're going to set up committees and advisory boards composed of learned men and skilled men from all countries and communities. I shall be President. And if my colleagues make difficulties and want to keep things I don't approve of, or refuse to keep things I do approve of, I shan't threaten to resign; I shall merely threaten to break off my engagement, and that will settle the matter. Well, good night to you."

The problem of preserving the past and present for the use of the future was so complex and difficult and all-important that Stella, with Alan's cooperation and sane counsel, now gave up everything else and devoted her time to the selection of her advisers. She sent for savants from all the different countries; she sent for the best engineers, economists, architects, scientists, art connoisseurs, medical men, and statesmen. But when various priests and bishops demanded representation on the boards, she refused, on the ground that they would only cause dissension.

"There will be room for only one religion in my new world," she said. "New ones may possibly be evolved from it in time, men being various and liking to hold opinions different from those of their neighbours, but I'm determined that we shall at least start with one. I was brought up a Christian and a Nonconformist, and though I became an agnostic at eighteen I would like my family to learn the simpler precepts of Christianity. If we were to attempt to keep alive all the many religions there are in the world, it would only confuse future generations quite unnecessarily, and make for endless trouble. What I want to hand down to posterity is a system of ethics founded on health, common sense, and an understanding of the law of cause and effect. You will say, some of you, that I am leaving out beauty, mystery, awe, and worship. People are bound to come to those quite naturally by studying nature, and the stars, and atoms, and the wonders of the human mind."

She wished, of course, she added, to preserve all the great religious writings for the use of scholars, but for the use of scholars only: "The new world will have plenty to do," she said. "It's the business of men to become as gods. They must learn to conquer space and time. They may even learn to conquer death."

I told her that I wouldn't live to see that day, nor did I wish to. "I look forward to my own death," I said, "once I have seen your offspring safely into the world, as a tired child looks forward to its bed."

And this was true. I had noticed of late that the effect of Evitalin was slightly decreasing, and for the first time I began to feel that I was growing old. It was more difficult for me to grasp at once what younger people were saying; my mind seemed almost wilfully inattentive, and little things began to matter to me, such as having a cup of tea at four-thirty, and sleeping after lunch. Noises disturbed me more; I began to recollect forgotten incidents of the past; and that impression of saying and doing and experiencing things for the second time became of more and more frequent occurrence.

Such a wild and fanatical interest was shown by the public in everything that was in any way connected with Stella that it seemed that Freddie might have to give up going to school – for Alan had had his way – owing to the crowds that collected wherever he went and the difficulty of getting about. I had so little use for Benglass nowadays that it had become his daily duty to accompany the boy to and from school, but he had several times been frightened that Freddie might meet with some accident, and he begged me to urge Stella to have him taught at the Palace. Alan solved the problem by buying a small new helicopter and getting in touch with a very expert young pilot, who now took Benglass's place and flew the boy to and from the school which was fifteen miles outside London – every day.

As for Stella herself, it was not thought safe for her to go beyond the grounds at all, so that her life was very confined and restricted. She too longed to use the helicopter, and fly to some place where she could run about freely without danger of molestation, but Mr. Hardy thought this far too risky.

"There is always the possibility," he said, "that you might be forced to come down owing to bad weather or some trouble with the receiver, and then there's no knowing what might happen." Alan agreed, and told her laughingly that she must wait until the nurseries were full. Then their lives would be their own, and they could come and go as they pleased.

"That we certainly can't," she said. "Do you think I would leave my children to the tender mercies of Mr. Hardy and the Cabinet?"

Great domes were now being built, with walls of immense thickness. Some were of steel and concrete, some of unbreakable glass, and they were to form a ring about the city. There were to be over two hundred of them, and in them was to be stored all the useful knowledge, all the accumulated wisdom of the world. They were to have small, heavy doors of chromium steel, the keys of which were to be in the keeping of Stella and Alan, to hand down to their descendants.

In one would be works of natural history; another would contain nothing but books on physics, with models and appliances used in the study of physics; the next would be for the students of chemistry, and so on. All the most important works on all the most important subjects were to be reprinted on a special sort of vellum-like paper, which, chemically treated, might be expected to withstand time or heat or cold. Thousands of educated men, professors and scholars of all sorts, volunteered to assist in the collecting and arranging of the material. One huge dome was to house the contents of the British Museum, and, while duplication was carefully avoided, objects of value and interest were to be sent from other countries all over the world.

About the preservation of books and music and works of art Stella allowed herself to be guided, but she resolutely refused to keep anything that dealt with the making of war. Books dealing with that subject in any form she rigidly excluded. At one of the committee meetings she found that Mr. Ossuldon, the Minister for War, had marshalled so powerful an opposition against her that she only got her way by threatening to remain single. I was there, and I shall never forget how she sprang to her feet and faced him, and told him that not only had he and his kind ruined the present world and brought it to an end, but that, not content with that, they were doing their best to bring about the doom of the next.

"You're incorrigible!" she cried. "Incorrigible! The marriage will not take place. I was a fool ever to think of it. When you've seen reason and common sense, if you ever do, let me know." And she left the room. Mr. Hardy was sent after her to bring her back, but it was a full hour before she could be persuaded to return, and by that time her opponents were ready to humble themselves and give way to her wishes. When they had apologized, she made a little speech.

"Our only enemies," she said, "will be the wild animals, which I suppose will greatly increase in numbers, and so some sort of firearm may be necessary as a protection, though I hope my descendants will learn to deal kindly with all wild creatures, and let them live in reservations of their own, and study them. But if men ever want machine guns and siege guns and dreadnoughts and bombs and submarines to use against one another, they will have to invent them for themselves. And I think," she added, "that the women of the future will see to it that they don't."

Alan pointed out to her one day, in my presence, and only half in earnest, that these threats to break off their engagement were a trifle humiliating for him. "Though I admit," he said, "that it's a most useful and powerful weapon."

"I thought we'd decided that our own personal feelings didn't matter," she answered. "In fact, I thought we'd decided not to have any personal feelings at all."

"Well," he said, "if that was the understanding, I'm afraid I've failed."

"I'm sorry, Alan," she said, "if it hurts your pride. But what can I do?"

"Pride!" he retorted. "If it hurt no more than that I wouldn't mind."

We were sitting in the garden, after lunch, in the shade of a huge old mulberry-tree. He got up and walked away, and after a moment's hesitation, Stella followed him. I don't know what happened then or what was said, but that night at dinner I thought they both looked much happier.

Moreover, the date of the wedding was put forward a few days. This caused some affectionate comment, and jokes were made very freely in the clubs, but Stella was quite indifferent to that sort of thing. She knew she could be.

She could never resist poking fun at Mr. Hardy and taking him to task, but underneath all her teasing I believe she was growing almost fond of him, and he was entirely devoted to her. Faults he certainly had, but he could never be disloyal once his allegiance was given, and, however much he disagreed with her, his admiration amounted almost to reverence. My own admiration was no less great, but to me she was like a daughter, and I grew to love her as one. Not a day passed without my taking either lunch or dinner and sometimes both – at the Palace, and I pitied all those millions who could see her only by television, who could hear her only from a distance and by air. To us, who were lucky enough to be close to her, her very presence was comforting and solacing beyond words. I often felt about her as I had felt as a child when I woke from a frightening dream and saw my mother in the room, busy about some small matter – quietly putting things away into a drawer, perhaps, or folding my clothes and laying them on a chair. Stella had only to come into a room to make the world seem no longer a chamber of protracted death, but a place that might once again be quickened by the spring.

The chief subject of discussion just at this time was, of course, the wedding, and the preparations for it. Although reluctant, at first, to be married in Westminster Abbey (not the Westminster Abbey of old – it and most of its contents had been destroyed in the war of 1950 – but as it had been rebuilt by Sir Wilfrid Lecomte), she gave way after some persuasion and told Mr. Hardy he could make what arrangements he pleased. He wasted no time. It should be the great day of the Archbishops and Bishops – the last of its kind – and he meant to see to it that it should also be a day of ceremony and splendour.

It was midsummer now, and the beautifying of London began. Preparations were made to accommodate tens of thousands of visitors, and many office buildings, and some of the big shops which were awaiting destruction, were turned into temporary hotels.

The decorations were planned with care and taste. No small flags were used along the route to the Abbey, only great banners, and these hung down from balconies and were draped along balustrades, and were suspended across the broad streets. For three or four days before the wedding, flowers poured into London from gardens all over the world, and planes were arriving so fast with fresh loads that it was difficult to know how to deal with them. They adorned all the routes into the city; from the Palace to the Abbey the streets were carpeted with them, and all the open spaces roundabout were flower-strewn and flower-decorated.

It was to be Stella's first public journey, and the greatest precautions were taken. No one was allowed to fly over London that day, and the city was ringed with our own police planes, ready to mount instantly at the first hint of danger.

Stella caught the popular excitement, and gave thought to her own appearance. She had an eye for effect, and she asked Stenka, the greatest dress designer of the time, to make her a replica of the dress worn by Queen Victoria at her wedding to Prince Albert. The result was pure Winterhalter and altogether feminine and charming. The immense skirts disguised the stockiness of her build, her smooth young shoulders rose delightfully from the low-cut bodice, and, at the final trying-on, which we were invited to attend, she made a picture that drew tears from my eyes, and quite overcame poor Stenka. He had tried to commit suicide after the death of the women, but had failed, and so had lived miserably on. Now he was in a sort of dressmaker's heaven, and the lustrous white satin became, in his hands, a sacred and symbolic thing.

If I have failed to say much about Alan, it is not because there is little to say but because there is too much, and I feel the need of putting down all that I can of what took place as quickly as I can. His tact and reasonableness saved many a difficult situation. His position, which was at once enviable and hateful, was also fantastic, even grotesque. Chance had placed him above all the men of the earth, but it was a role which not only lacked dignity but lent itself all too easily to jesting comment. He played it, nevertheless, with grace and good humour and with admirable self-control. Fortunately neither he nor Stella were difficult people to get on with. I was afraid at first that Stella's natural bluntness and downrightness might sometimes offend him, but the enormous demands made upon her patience and her intelligence had increased her powers of understanding, and she knew better now when to give way and when to stand firm. Indeed, it seemed to me that mentally she added a cubit to her stature every day.

There was a cold and rainy period in the early part of July, but, as the great day approached, the weather turned hot and bright, so that the banners dried and the flowers were only freshened by the final shower. The Palace was in a ferment; in fact, the whole of London hummed with excitement. Men had lighter hearts, I think, than at any time since the great disaster, and not a boy old enough to be taken to see the wedding procession but must have looked forward to the day with almost unbearable impatience.

Then, on the night before the wedding, a most alarming and tragic thing happened – a thing that might, indeed, have ended in worse than tragedy; in complete disaster.

The excitement had unsettled everyone a little, I think. The Palace guard had perhaps been celebrating; at any rate, the sentries were not as watchful as they should have been or the thing could never have happened. I had dined at the Palace as usual; it was a more or less family dinner-party, and included, besides our hostess, Mr. Hardy, Alan, the boy, myself, and only one other visitor: Sir Derek Sambourne, the Astronomer Royal.

Stella had been discussing with him the plans for a great new planetarium to be built outside London. There were many of these on the Continent, but the only one of any size in England had been destroyed in 1950 and had never been rebuilt.

People – because of the smoky atmosphere of England in the past, perhaps – had not learnt to interest themselves in the stars, nor had they been much encouraged to do so. Stella believed that if the planetarium were built at this time it might be very popular with boys and young men, as well as highly instructive. Her own small observatory in the Palace grounds had been finished some time before – it was a small circular building resembling a Greek temple – and she visited it every fine evening. She was going to visit it with Sir Derek this evening, but before going out she had to keep an appointment with the microphone, for she had promised to give a short talk on the air at nine-thirty.

"I am very happy tonight," she said. "I am not going to think too much about the future. I want to be happy for a while just as other women have been happy; I want to forget my unique and awful and lonely position, and live for a little, not as an ancestress, but simply as a bride. Bless you all, and thank you for everything you have done to make tomorrow the greatest day of my life. I shan't forget it, I promise you. Good night."

Mr. Hardy, who was very tired, excused himself early and went to his bedroom – in Downing Street, Stella supposed, but actually in the West Tower. Alan, Freddie, and I settled down to a game of rummy in the library, and Stella and Sir Derek went to the observatory. The windows of the room occupied by Mr. Hardy looked out on that side. It was a very fine night indeed, warm and windless and already faintly lighted by the moon, which was just rising. I imagine that Mr. Hardy put on his dressing gown and read for a little while, and then, before going to bed, put out the lights and went to the window. There he no doubt saw a thing which must have angered and distressed him, and roused all his indignation.

It was strictly against the rules for Stella to be alone in the grounds of the Palace at any time, but especially at night, and he must have seen her come out of the observatory with Sir Derek, and, instead of returning with him to the Palace, bid him good night there, and stroll off alone across the lawn towards the lake, above which the moon, delayed by distant buildings, had just risen. Sir Derek, instead of coming into the library, went straight through the hall and out by the front door. My ears are fairly sharp, and I thought at the time that I heard it close, but was not sure. Old Venning, one of the servants, brought in some drinks on a tray just after that and went out again. Mr. Hardy, without stopping to put on his clothes, and wishing, I have no doubt, to scold Stella then and there before his anger had cooled, must have hurried down the stairs and out into the garden just as he was.

Suddenly we heard him shouting at the top of his voice, and the sound froze our blood. "Help! Help!" he screamed. "For God's sake, help!"

Alan ran to the open window, stepped on the sill, and jumped twenty feet down to a flower bed beneath it. I told Freddie to stay where he was and went down the stairs and into the garden as fast as my legs would carry me. In the middle of the lawn, half-way between the Palace and the observatory, I saw a dark object touched with shining metal, and surmounted by a propeller which was still whirring noiselessly. Two men were struggling in it, and running towards it, carrying Stella in their arms, were two others. The guard came tumbling out, sentries came running, there were shouts and confusion; I heard Stella crying out, above the hubbub, "No killing! No killing!" I saw the guards strike down the men who had been carrying her; I saw one of the dark figures in the machine flung out and seized, and the other, Alan, leap out and run to Stella. When I reached them she was assuring him she was unhurt and asking for Mr. Hardy. And then we saw a dark form lying in the shade of some bushes. Stella, with a cry of grief and pity, knelt down beside it. He must have been shot, soundlessly, as he gave the warning, and had fallen forward on his face. His dressing-gown was soaked with blood, and his eyes were closed. I took his wrist. The pulse was barely perceptible, and, baring his breast, we saw that he had been shot above the heart. We did all that could be done and made him as comfortable as we could there, for he was dying, and to move him would only have been to hasten the end. Stella was sobbing and saying, "Mr. Hardy, Mr. Hardy, speak to me! Say you forgive me!" He opened his eyes presently and whispered, "The end of the world, for me." Stella lifted his hand and laid it against her cheek. She kept repeating, "Thank you, oh, thank you, thank you! Dearest, dearest Mr. Hardy, what shall I do without you?"

He only spoke once more. It was to whisper, "No change ... the wedding, tomorrow ... no change. As if I were there ... I will try to be there." At the end she covered her face with her hands, and Alan led her away. The garden was quiet now, and in the moonlight that flooded it the strange machine seemed to rest as lightly on the lawn as a butterfly, or a silvery moth. A sentry stood motionless beside it. The three prisoners had been taken to the guardhouse and all was peaceful once more, and nothing more peaceful than Mr. Hardy's face.

Stella was suffering from remorse as well as from grief. She kept repeating, "I made fun of him. I called him the man of blood, and now he's shed his own for me. He died for me, and I made fun of him."

"To die for you," Alan said, "isn't a death any man would shrink from, Mr. Hardy least of all."

She said he was to lie at the Palace, and when I told her he had had his own room there, and had never left it for a night since her coming, she almost broke down again. I sent her and the over-excited Freddie to bed – the boy had followed me out, in spite of my instructions, and had seen a good deal – and Alan went to speak to the captain of the guard.

Later, when he came back, I went to Stella's bedroom and knocked softly on her door. She was awake, and I was able to tell her who the men were. We had already guessed their nationality, and, though they denied that they were acting for their Government, one of them had been unwise enough to keep a scrap of paper which gave them the lie.

"I won't have them executed," she said. "What would be the good of that? There are millions of others. They shall be flown over their own territory and dropped with parachutes. I have one death on my conscience, and I don't want any more."

I gave her a dose of Euthanol, and presently she was sleeping as peacefully as though nothing had happened.

The wedding-day was a day of double rejoicing, for when men heard of the attempt that had been made to carry Stella off – an attempt that had so narrowly been frustrated – they went wild with relief and joy. There was talk of making war on the offending nation, and there were undoubtedly many thousands of men who would have welcomed a war as an exciting change from the boredom and aimlessness of their daily lives. Before dressing for the ceremony, however, Stella decided to give a short talk on the air.

"I have lost a dear, devoted friend," she said, "and I shall miss him more than words can say. It is thanks to him that I am here today, for he first saw the danger and gave the alarm. He had great qualities; he had faults, too, but he was a great man, both in his living and in his dying. Today we must rejoice – it was his dying wish – but tomorrow we will mourn him as he de serves to be mourned.

"In the grounds of the Palace is a wonderful new machine, which rises and descends with only the faintest whirring sound. A child could fly it – my small nephew has already been up in it this morning. None of us heard it last night, and so we were taken by surprise, but we will not be taken by surprise again. The guard will be doubled – trebled, if necessary. There is no danger. And let us hear no talk of war. I had promised one of my daughters to a child of a certain nation on the condition that that nation behaved as a good neighbour should. It has not done so, and my daughter shall have another husband. I want no Cains or robbers among my sons-in-law. Now I must go and put on my wedding-dress."

Nowadays, when Stella spoke, her voice was everywhere amplified, such was the desire of all men to hear her. Wherever people came and went, wherever they worked or played or rested, she talked to them. It was very strange at first to be walking along some busy street and suddenly to hear her voice at one's ear, but we had grown accustomed to it now and could not do without it. She was the Universal Woman, and her voice the voice of Womankind. She was hope; she was the future; she was life.

She had asked that men should not wear military uniforms at her wedding. "Becoming though they are," she said, "and splendid, I don't wish to be reminded on such a day of what led to the death of all other women. I would like you to devise for yourselves, instead, fancy-dress costumes which will make the scene gay and colourful and give it more the air of a fête."

The result far exceeded anyone's expectations. Men entered into the scheme with zest and enthusiasm, and the sight was unforgettable. There were tens of thousands who wore Elizabethan doublet and hose; others who dressed like Cavaliers; many more who decked themselves out like Balkan peasants or gypsies or Italian organ-grinders or Greeks or Romans or Indians or Cossacks. It was a city of revellers. It outdid Venice in carnival time. It outdid anything I have ever seen or imagined. And if these were sunset splendours, as indeed they were, you may believe that they were none the less beautiful and touching and significant for being so.

Stella had very definite views as to the form the wedding procession should take, and Ministers and advisers talked and argued themselves hoarse in vain. She refused to go to the Abbey by car or by coach. She would walk, and she would go in no other way. Neither would she have any other escort than eight pages in white, of whom, she announced, Freddie would be the eldest. She would walk slowly, in her wedding dress, the boys holding up her train, from the Palace to the Abbey. If they feared for her safety, they could place as many policemen as they pleased along the route to keep back the crowds. That was their affair. If they feared that she might soil her skirts, let carpets be laid down. Walk she would.

Needless to say, she won in the end, though some were in despair. Alan was on her side, and was for letting her do exactly as she pleased. If any madman should have designs on her life, he said, it would make little difference whether she walked or rode. But today of all days, he believed, no man on earth could wish her ill; not even the most evil could fail to be moved and stirred by such an occasion.

Representatives of foreign nations, men who had in some way been of service, and men renowned in letters, the arts, or the sciences – all these were invited to the Abbey, and wisely took their seats before nine o'clock, for since early morning the streets had been packed by gaily dressed crowds, and the police had all they could do to keep a way open and the route clear.

Stella was to walk from the Palace down the Mall through the great archway at the bottom that had been built to commemorate the men, women, and children of London who had lost their lives in the Twenty Days' War, and so down Whitehall to the Abbey. Banners waved on either hand and above her head; the route was carpeted with flowers – the warm and sunny air was heavy with their scent.

The Palace gates opened promptly at ten, and the little procession started. Imagine, if you can, how the sight moved, how it drove to a frenzy of gladness and worship, those masculine crowds. Picture it if you can – the world's only surviving woman, setting out on foot in that spreading white satin gown to meet her bridegroom. The eight little pages held up the great train and kept in step with her all the way. She moved slowly, smiling as she went, quite deafened, I expect, by that astounding roar of voices, looking with friendly unfrightened eyes at those dense and living walls. I wish I could have seen her pass. I wish that I could have watched her during every step of that journey. (I saw her set out. So did Alan, and then we left the Palace by a back door, and were driven in a special police car to the Abbey by way of Victoria.) But I can shut my eyes and see her now, with the white satin shining in the sun; the lovely, billowing, gleaming skirts taking on light and shadows as she moved; no jewels anywhere, and on her head a wreath of white gardenias. I don't know how she stood the frenzied homage of the crowd; I don't know how she bore it or what kept the little boys – all of them, except Freddie, under ten – from bursting into frightened tears. I imagine that long before they reached the Abbey they had grown accustomed to the uproar, had tasted and tested and schooled themselves to bear that wild good will, that frantic worship. So slow was their progress that I guessed, sitting there, my watch hidden in my palm, that she stopped more than once to give her hand to some old man, perhaps, whose tears moved her unbearably, and paused to speak and thank those seas of well-wishers, though not a word of hers could have been heard by them. At last she drew near, and the shouting beat upon our ears. She was reaching the end of her journey, and as the noise increased we marvelled that it could grow still louder. Even the great organ failed to drown it, and only when the little procession reached the great porch and entered the Abbey, and the doors were closed, was that roar, that almost tangible body of sound, softened and then stilled. And as Mr. Devray came up the aisle with Stella on his arm, the little pages lost some of their awed solemnity, and, as they followed her, dared to smile at one another and look about them.

Alan was waiting at the altar steps with young Philip Devray, his best man, beside him. I was sitting in one of the front pews, and when the organ began to play the Wedding March from *Lohengrin* – Mr. Hardy had begged hard for this – I looked at Alan's face and saw that for him the suspense and the waiting had been almost unendurable. And now he had still to endure Stella's long slow walk up the aisle, the emotional trembling of the Archbishop's hands and lips, the sobbing of some of the congregation, the sight, at last, of the bride. He had to turn to her, moved and keyed up to a high tension though he was, a face in which she could see only confidence, gladness, and love.

I was close beside them, and I saw their eyes meet. It seemed to me that their children might have been born in that look. And it seemed to me, too, for I think my brain had been clarified by my own emotions, that one of the great things we had forgotten – or had we never learnt it? – was the mystery that lay behind birth, behind personality, behind life and death. And I thought that in such a tiny world as would come after us, life would perhaps become a more valued thing, would perhaps be known for the mystery and the wonder that it is. Men would no longer be seen as trees walking, to be hewn down, but as worlds walking, worlds in finitely complex, unique, and inviolate.

And at that moment I saw each living thing in its two-fold role – as a cell or minute segment in some vast organism of which we perceive only the faintest shadow; and as a universe with its own stars and galaxies and immensities and its own tiny marvels, the infinitely small bound up with the infinitely great, and all presided over by a hopeful, lonely, anxious, and unique intelligence, a unique awareness, complete in itself, like no other, necessary to itself, and never to be repeated. "I," in short; the great enigma. And when we slay, who knows what we slay? Who knows? And until we feel this mystery in our bones and in our blood, feel and worship this uniqueness first of all in our brother and then in ourselves, what are we but idiot children with the idiot's pleasure in destruction; obscene, swaggering, senseless little monsters? Stella felt this in her bones and in her blood; Alan felt it. I knew that they were fit to start a new world because they knew, intuitively, something of the sacredness of life, something of the mystery of intelligence. And now these two, who had kindness in their hearts, would marry and multiply. Perhaps in time there might even yet be a race of men not too sunk in their own stupidity to learn with pride their own infinite potentialities. So I hoped, so I believed, sitting there in the Abbey, blinded by my own tears.

Their responses were clear and firm, and I was glad, for they were listened to in China, in Labrador, in Persia, everywhere. The Archbishop made a short address. He well knew the immense significance of that moment, knew that he was joining one epoch, which had all but ended, to another still unborn, and he wished to speak fittingly.

"Teach your little world to love," he said. "Oh, teach it to love!"

I wondered what Stella was thinking. She admired and respected the Archbishop as a man, I knew, but her heart was in a better place than his, for his was too much concerned with pomp and dignity and grandeur and the pride of Establishment, and hers was naturally and simply good.

He said that the saving of Stella's life, both from the universal death of women and from the danger to which she had been exposed the night before, were no fortuitous circumstances, but part of a Divine Plan. (I think that Stella would have answered to this that if the saving of her life were part of a Divine Plan, so must the war and the disease have been. She would have said, I imagine, that if there were indeed a Divine Plan – and there might well be – it was one which few of us had seen and recognized, and the rest had blindly and ignorantly strayed from.)

"How can we doubt it?" the Archbishop asked. "How can we doubt that a merciful Creator, of His loving kindness, has given the world one more opportunity? He has chosen you, Stella Morrow, and you, Alan Holderness, to be His instruments. Great is your destiny – unspeakably great. As great as your privilege. Your descendants may be as gods; they may make for themselves a world beyond our poor imaginings."

The crowds had been absolutely silent during the ceremony; they too had been listening to the service; but as soon as it was over, and the bells rang out, the shouting and cheering began once more. As Alan and Stella got into a car and drove slowly back to the Palace, the roar followed them. Now the crowd pressed on to the Palace itself, and looking out on it from the balcony, it seemed that there was not space for one more person anywhere, and all the great mass was in motion, arms waving, hats being tossed into the air. Again and again and yet again Stella, sometimes alone, sometimes accompanied by Alan, went out and spoke to them. She was bewildered by their fanatical, passionate interest in her, their hunger to see the one small being who could carry forward the vital spark.

"Oh, you strange creatures!" I heard her cry out, once. "So careless of life and of the world, so eager for it to continue! Who can understand you?"

In the evening the crowds were still there, and showed no sign of dispersing and going home. The whole population of London and of countless other places was giving itself up to revelry and rejoicing, and meant, we could see, to make a night of it.

We dined quietly at the Palace, the Devrays, father and son, myself, Stella, Alan, and the boy. The latter was stupefied with exhaustion, and had promised to go to bed as soon as dinner was over. Out of respect for Mr. Hardy there were to be no functions, and we drank the health of the bride and the groom very quietly. There would be little change at the Palace. Alan was sharing Stella's apartments now, instead of living with me, and, apart from that, everything was as before. Of necessity their lives would be restricted – they were not their own, to do with as they pleased – but there would be much to occupy them, and there was a whole future world to plan for. We had heard that very morning that Professor Greeves, of Cambridge, had succeeded in deciphering the whole of Dr. Hummel's notes, and believed that the secret of the stain was now accessible to the world. Almost simultaneously, another scientist, a biologist, was reported to have perfected a serum which, acting upon certain glands in childhood, developed spiritual powers of a very high order, and could even, in time, change the most bestial adult into a being with spiritual faculties and a desire for good. Alan had already asked the biologist to come to the Palace, and he and Stella were arranging with Mr. Devray for tests to be made at some of the prisons. They were discussing this and similar matters after dinner, and feeling, suddenly, a little faint, I left them on some pretext and sat for a while in the garden. There was little peace there, however, because of the noise made by the crowd beyond the gates, so I presently went up to Mr. Hardy's room, feeling that it would be restful to sit with the dead. I told his old servant, who was watching by him, that I would relieve him for a little, and I took the chair he had left. It was peaceful enough there, and I could think over all that had happened. It seemed to me that I was not needed any longer; that my work, like Mr. Hardy's, was done. I had promised Stella to go on taking Evitalin though its effects were noticeably less than they had been until after the birth of her first two girls, and I meant to keep my promise, though there were many quite as competent to see them safely into the world as myself. I was so tired tonight, however, that I would gladly have been released from my promise. The excitements and alarms of the night before, the death of Mr. Hardy, the emotions of the day, had affected me far more than I had realized, and as I looked at the serene face upon the bed I had less of pity in my heart for him than of envy. He had died bravely. He had been, at that moment, indispensable. He was younger than I, and had not yet begun to take Evitalin, but he was never a strong man and had always suffered from moods and fits of depression. He was a true representative of that past which was now to die – no, he was a representative of a still earlier past and had survived into this one because he was able to dominate it.

His death and the death of the world I knew seemed somehow bound up together. My eyelids closed as I sat there; sleep and weariness pressed them down. I struggled to open them, but, when I did, a grey curtain seemed to come between me and what I looked at. I felt cold; cold and old and unhappy. My spirit seemed to be struggling and fluttering within me. I think I lost consciousness completely, and when I came to myself I was rubbing my cold hands. I looked down at them, and they were no longer the wrinkled hands of an old man but the smooth, strong hands of a man in the prime of life. For a while I hung perilously and fearfully between two worlds, unable to come wholly alive in either, then slowly the grey mist cleared and I saw that I was in the top-floor room of the Society of Inquirers in Campden Hill Gardens, sitting, in the dusk, beside the prone body of Spero, the medium.

I had had the most amazing experience ever given, I think, to any man. I wanted to tell Spero about it. I wanted to tell the whole world about it. I heard the voices of women outside the door. Miss Ongar, the secretary of the society, and another girl who sometimes helped her, were talking together on the landing. They were speaking quietly, and presently they went down the stairs and I heard them no longer. Women's voices! I was living in a normal world, a world of living women, a world unconscious of the way it was drifting. I wanted to shout down to them, "Be careful! Do something! Do something!" I longed to ask Spero if this experience of fifty years hence were real, if it were actually the coming fate of the world that I had witnessed – that I had experienced – or some "What-Might-Be," lying within the great lap of time but never, please heaven! never to be encountered by us. I was afraid to wake him too suddenly, afraid to bring him back too soon from whatever hinterland he lingered in. I got up and walked about the darkening room, haunted, possessed, by the world from which I had just come. With only a little effort, I felt, I could return to the library where Stella and Alan sat talking with Mr. Devray and his son, who would get up and say good night as soon as I returned. Surely I could go back! Surely I could see Stella again! Only a moment ago I had caught her eyes as I left the room, and she had looked at me anxiously, because she had seen how tired I was. Surely I had only to walk out of the room where Mr. Hardy lay and along the corridor, and then down the marble stairs to the library where they were all waiting for me.

I went to the door and saw the shabby landing, the narrow stairs of the house on Campden Hill. I heard the sound of the lift coming up, and, feeling too uncertain of myself and too shaken to meet anyone just then, I returned to the room and to the motionless Spero. But there was a cautious knock on the door, and I said, "Come in," and switched on the light.

Dr. Bianchetti opened it. He was a big, striking-looking man of fifty or so, lively, vital, with brilliant eyes and large, handsome features. He looked from me to Spero. "How is he?" he asked. "I have come to see."

"Still unconscious," I told him. I brushed my hand over my eyes. "I've just come back from a long journey myself."

He was holding Spero's wrist. "Get help, my friend," he said quickly. "Call the secretary. We must work fast, you and I, or he will never come back. Perhaps it is already too late."

We worked over Spero for a long time, Bianchetti and I. He never came back. I blamed myself, as we left the house at last, for having allowed him to make this final experiment, but Bianchetti entirely exonerated me.

"My dear fellow," he said, in his rapid, slightly Italianate English, "what Ugolino Spero wished to do, he did. He was stronger than you. Stronger than me. He was a great man, a wonderful man, and a great mystery to materialists like myself. Now I want to know, was the experiment successful?"

"Incredibly successful," I said. "But there was a question I longed to ask him. Everything hangs on the answer, and now I shall never know what that answer is."

I have only one thing more to add. I am very tired. I can hardly keep my eyes open any longer, for it is now after five, and I have been writing since half-past eight. This is what I want to tell you. Before sitting down to write the account you have just read, I rang up a cousin of mine who knows Gloucestershire well and has friends living near Stroud. These friends are large landowners, and I knew that my cousin often stayed with them there. I asked him if he knew of a family named Morrow tenant farmers, I thought they might be living in the district. He said the name meant nothing to him, but that he could easily find out all about them by ringing up his friends. This he obligingly did, and a few minutes later he telephoned to say that there was a couple named Morrow, fairly young, with no children as yet, living on a hundred-acre farm in the parish of Wonnup.

Stella's grandparents? It seems more than likely.

CONTRIBUTORS

Susan Ertz (1887–1985) was an Anglo-American novelist known for blending romance, social satire and philosophical reflection. Born in Surrey, England, to American parents, she spent much of her childhood in the USA before settling in Britain. Her breakthrough came with *Madame Claire* (1923). Among her most notable works is *Woman Alive* (1936), a speculative novel about the last woman surviving a global plague, praised for its originality and feminist undertones. Over a long career, Ertz explored women's independence and moral dilemmas, leaving behind a body of fiction that remains both popular and thought-provoking.

Graham Norton began his broadcasting career as comedian and panellist on the BBC Radio Four show *Loose Ends* in the early 1990s. He has hosted various radio and TV shows, including the multi-BAFTA-winning *The Graham Norton Show*. Norton has written two memoirs, *So Me* and *The Life and Loves of a He Devil*. In 2016, he published his debut novel, *Holding*, followed by the bestselling *A Keeper* which tells of a New York-based academic returning to her Irish hometown after the death of her mother. Norton's third novel, *Home Stretch*, is a moving exploration of guilt and the search for a place to belong. He discovered Susan Ertz's novel *Madame Claire* at a church fete in West Cork, and was instantly smitten with her work.

Tom Gauld was born in Aberdeen and studied at Edinburgh College of Art and The Royal College of Art. He is a cartoonist and illustrator with weekly comic strips in *The Guardian* and *New Scientist*. His comics have been published in the *New York Times* and on the cover of *The New Yorker*. He is the author of *Goliath*, *You're All Just Jealous of My Jetpack*, *Mooncop*, *Baking with Kafka* (winner of an Eisner Award), *Department of Mind-Blowing Theories*, *Revenge of the Librarians* and *Physics for Cats*. He lives with his family in London.

MANDERLEY PRESS TITLES

Edinburgh: Picturesque Notes **by Robert Louis Stevenson**
Introduced by Alexander McCall Smith
Illustrated by Iain McIntosh

The Armourer's House **by Rosemary Sutcliff**
Introduced by Lara Maiklem
Illustrated by Isabel Greenberg

Appointment with Venus **by Jerrard Tickell**
Introduced by Rosa Rankin-Gee
Illustrated by Edward Bawden

The Fly on the Wheel **by Katherine Cecil Thurston**
Introduced by Megan Nolan
Illustrated by Kathi Burke

Letter from New York **by Helene Hanff**
Introduced by Jean Hanff Korelitz
Illustrated by Bruce Eric Kaplan

China Court **by Rumer Godden**
Introduced by Linda Grant
Illustrated by Emily Maude

The House in Cornwall **by Noel Streatfeild**
Introduced by Lucy Mangan
Illustrated by Elly Jahnz

Tales of London Town **by Joan Aiken**
Introduced by Kiran Millwood Hargrave
Illustrated by Annabel Pearl

***Florence: Ordeal by Water* by Kathrine Kressmann Taylor**
Introduced by Vanessa Nicolson
Illustrated by Agnesbic

***Washington Square* by Henry James**
Introduced by Colm Tóibín
Illustrated by Rose Wong

Mary Shelley in Bath
Introduced by Fiona Sampson
Illustrated by Eleanor Macnair

***Sun Horse, Moon Horse* by Rosemary Sutcliff**
Introduced by Tiffany Francis-Baker
Illustrated by Isabel Greenberg

***The Strange House* by Raymond Briggs**
Introduced by Chris Riddell
Illustrated by Raymond Briggs

***Underfoot in Show Business* by Helene Hanff**
Introduced by Jean Hanff Korelitz
Illustrated by Bruce Eric Kaplan

***Woman Alive* by Susan Ertz**
Introduced by Graham Norton
Illustrated by Tom Gauld